The Cosantóirí

ZOE JONES

www.srlpublishing.co.uk

SRL Publishing Ltd
42 Braziers Quay
Bishop's Stortford
Herts, CM23 3YW

First published worldwide by SRL Publishing in 2019

ISBN: 978-0-9957323-5-3

To Jessica Leeds, and Katharina Gasper I give my gratitude and thanks for your most excellent proof reading, your honesty, and your friendship.

To Josh Waller, Niamh Breslin, Madeleine Rees, and Courtney Martin-Luce thank you for being my support system, and my family away from home.

To my readers, thank you! I hope The Cosantóirí brings you the same joy that it brought me to write.

I would like to thank Mum and Dad for encouraging my creativity and my desire to learn, for queuing up at midnight to buy me the newest book releases, and for loving me just as I am. This book would not have been possible without the both of you.

Thank you to my family and friends, near and far, old and new, for filling my life with adventures, memories, and stories to tell.

CHAPTER 1

"TRAINS ARE FUNNY, IF you think about it," mused Alexandra as she nervously tapped her fingers on the luggage handle of her suitcase. The incessant drum beat thudding in time with her anxious heart as she shuffled on the spot to stay warm.

"I mean, we're all crammed into this gross metal sweatbox with complete strangers. Strangers who, I would like to point out, have no regard for well-established personal space boundaries."

Micah rolled his eyes as if he'd heard this rant before. "I did offer to drive you, you know? But as I recall, you declined."

The dark tight curls atop Micah's head bounced slightly as he dipped his head pointedly towards Alexandra, his eyebrow raised in sync. His hands were hidden in the warmth of the green parka he was sporting, but Alexandra was certain that if it wasn't frostbite warning, cold outside he would have wagged his finger in her face with his usual sass.

Alexandra forced a grin with no feeling. "Friends don't let friends slack off work to drive them halfway across the country in a beat up truck that probably wouldn't make it back".

Micah made a barely audible sound that Alexandra was sure disguised a very mature '*whatever*'. A loud rumble began to rise from the ground, travelling up through Alexandra's bones and rattling her core. Snow slumped from the station roof onto the tracks from the vibrations.

"Now, don't be hating on my truck just because you have to sit in this petri dish of delight for five hours," Micah mocked playfully as he gestured towards the approaching train.

Alexandra could feel the stress and anxiety from the last few days threatening to rise up and explode all over the crowded platform. Micah must have sensed the dread she was feeling, because he uncharacteristically embraced her in a warm hug and simply stated, "You're gonna be okay, A".

Micah was the only human she let get away with calling her A; from him it felt sweet and comforting, but from anyone else, not so much. Alexandra could remember the night she had first met Micah; they had both been invited to the fresher's party, a night to welcome all the newbie's into the college fold. Alexandra could recall how nervous she was, walking into a room filled with strangers, most of them already black-out drunk. She had been in the midst of an uncomfortable interaction with one of the boys who was hosting the party, when Micah had cut in. "I can already assure you it's a definite no." Micah had stated, his tone filled with a mild annoyance.

"Dude. I never asked you." The drunk senior had retorted after them as Micah had led her to the garden.

"Who knew college would be filled with just as many douche bags as high school," Micah laughed. They had spent the night laughing at the drunken masses, and bonding over a shared brand of sarcasm and wit. Micah and Alexandra had been almost inseparable ever since. They had been through every bad date, every emotional *'I can't do it'* break down, and every life stress together. Alexandra was the one who introduced Micah to his first serious boyfriend, and Micah was the one who would drop everything to help her - no questions asked. Just like today. As the train halted at the station, Alexandra left the safety of Micah's hug, flashed him a friendly smile of gratitude, and boarded the train. Each step was an uncomfortable effort as she battled with the crowds to start her journey back home. Alexandra dumped her beat-up, ragged suitcase onto the luggage rack. The rustic exterior of her well-used case was a stark contrast to its fellow travel buddies, all shiny and new in various neon shades.

After squeezing her way past a coach full of passengers, she scooted into her window seat, hoping that she would not be subjected to a travel buddy of her own. This was not a journey made for small talk, for hearing the life story of some eccentric elderly gentleman you hope you're never going to see again, or for hearing the first world problems of the teenagers cackling away at the table seat behind you. No. Not today. Today was for headphones in, music up loud, and watching the trees and lakes pass you by. Today was for taking calming breaths to steady a pounding heart.

Alexandra stared wistfully out of the window as she thought back on the events of the last two days. What a whirlwind they had been. Well not really a whirlwind, more like a hurricane or a tropical storm she thought. Her heart began to pound again as calming breaths turned into heavy pants, and tears threatened to blur her usually warm brown eyes. Nothing about today could constitute *'usual'*.

[24 hours ago]

A loud buzzing sound vibrated on the bedside table as Alexandra awoke, the haze of the morning concealing the extent of what was sure to be a horrendous hangover by noon. Rising to a seated position, Alexandra untangled her legs from the bed sheets until she was perched on the edge of the bed. A wild mass of thick black curls tickled her shoulders as she wiped the sleep from her eyes and reached for her phone, the cool morning air made her shiver now that she was outside of the protection of the duvet.

"Who calls this early on a weekend?" said an unfamiliar, strained voice from the crumpled mound of bedding, startling Alexandra in her dazed morning state. Alexandra rose to her feet, inspecting her bed-mate with curiosity as she took a step backwards, away from last night's booze-fuelled, clouded judgement.

"Shit!" Alexandra exclaimed as she stubbed her toe on a half full beer bottle, most of which was now soaking into the cream carpet.

The duvet shifted as the voice revealed itself to belong to a sweet, soft-faced, blonde with porcelain pale skin.

"Sorry!" Alexandra whispered - although at this point she realised whispering was no longer necessary. Alexandra continued to stumble backwards towards the bedroom door, away from the woman in her bed.

"I have to, to uh, uh, take this...this phone... this call, phone call." she spluttered as she made a hasty retreat from the bedroom.

She made a mental note to feel the embarrassment of this moment later, and for the hundredth time made a pact to never do tequila shots again. With the soft click of the door closing, Alexandra made her way across the lounge to the window seat, sparing a longing glance at the tea on the kitchen side table as she passed. What she'd kill for a cup of sweet, milky tea right now. Looking back at the impatiently vibrating phone in her hand she cleared her throat and answered.

"Hey, Aunt Alondra, do you know how early it is?".

"Sorry, Miss Alex. It's Wyatt." the deep, gravelly voice revealed; a sombre air to his words.

Alexandra's face contorted in confusion and her brow furrowed as she replied.

"Wyatt? Why are you calling on Aunt Alondra's phone? You have your own, you know?" She pushed her fingers against her temple, trying to massage the tired confusion and pulsing headache away.

"I would have preferred not to tell you over the phone, Miss Alex, or to be telling you this at all."

Wyatt's tone was glum and reserved as he took an unnaturally long pause.

"I don't understand, is something wrong? Wyatt?". Alexandra rolled her eyes. "We need to work on your telephone manner, Wyatt. Long segments of silence don't really translate via telephone. Just tell me what's going on, you're making me nervous!".

Wyatt's voice was softer as he spoke this time. "Yes, something is quite wrong, my dear...Miss Alondra is no longer with us. What I mean to say is, that she died. Last night. Miss Alex, I am so sorry."

The room pitched as Alexandra's head began to spin dizzyingly, her ears ringing as if someone had clapped their hands over them, hard. The echo of Wyatt's voice felt distant as Alexandra fought to control her breathing. It felt as if she had just been dumped into ice cold water and was desperately trying not to drown. Her heart hurt, the weight threatening to overwhelm her. Guilt rose as she flashed back to snippets of the wild night before; rows of shots, dancing to the local live band, drinks spilling, people shouting and singing, flirty glances, and flashing lights.

"Miss Alex. Miss Alex! Are you still there, Miss Alex?"

Wyatt's concerned tone cut through the crashing waves of emotion like a life raft lifting her from the water's icy clutches. Alexandra felt the warmth of tears streaming down her lightly freckled cheeks, her voice cracking as she spoke.

"Yes. Yes, I'm still here." The regret of her sarcastic tone, and annoyance at being awoken so early, was clear. "What...what happened? How...I just...I don't understand!".

"It is difficult to explain, Miss Alex. It is not something I can tell you over the phone, but something I must explain in person. Here, at Chadwick Manor. I have booked a train for you, and the details should be in your inbox shortly."

Wyatt's tone was apologetic, but certain. It was clear that Wyatt had no intention of revealing any more to Alexandra until they were in the same room. Alexandra hung up the phone, her body frozen in place slumped on the window seat, her eyes staring ahead without seeing. The bedroom door clicked open, the sound barely audible over the swirling thoughts in Alexandra's head. The blonde. Alexandra had completely forgotten about the blonde in her bed. Hastily wiping tears from her face Alexandra lifted her head locking eyes with the blonde.

"Hey. You sounded upset so I thought I would come and make you tea. I mean it's basically a hug in a mug when you get the good stuff, and my nana always says tea can solve the world's problems. She's a little crazy, but still it's kind of a nice sentiment I guess. Plus I always like a nice warm cuppa when I'm sad. Sorry, I'm totally rambling and you have that face like you're worried you might offend me if you ask me my name. It's Casey, Casey Ray. Nice to meet you again, Alexandra."

Casey beamed a winning smile filled with kindness and sincerity. Alexandra couldn't help but smile back as if Casey's kind soul was contagious.

"Nice to meet you, again, too. I'm sure I must have mentioned that tequila is not a tool that facilitates memory storage for me." Alexandra grinned apologetically. "Tea would be nice though." She added hastily to the end of her sentence.

Alexandra could feel the numbness thawing slowly, but the pain in her chest felt like it might never leave her.

"Earl Grey, milky with one sugar?" Casey asked.

"Yes," responded Alexandra a hint of surprise in her voice.

"I take my barista duties very seriously, it's my job to know my customers' orders. Especially the cute regulars." Casey winked cheekily, and turned towards the kitchen.

7

"So what's got you so upset? I mean I wouldn't usually pry, but I figure I've seen you in your birthday suit so personal questions are acceptable."

Taken aback by Casey's matter-of-fact tone, Alexandra could feel the heat rising in her cheeks. It was not very often Alexandra became embarrassed; in fact, she took pride in her ability to be fairly infallible in awkward situations. She certainly had enough experience being an all-round awkward human - the last 24 years worth of experience - that such interactions barely fazed her anymore. But there was something different about this moment; it didn't feel awkward, it felt significant in some way.

Alexandra shook her head and rubbed her hands across her face, her grief and hung-over state were clearly toying with her sense of logic. Casey turned around with two fresh mugs of tea, the delicate aroma of bergamot filling the room. Alexandra breathed in the calming scent as she took the mug from Casey, an accidental brush of her hand against Casey's making Alexandra's heart beat faster and her cheeks blush again. The smell of Earl Grey grounded her, it always had. Alexandra breathed in the warm scent once more before she answered Casey's question.

"I just found out my Aunt, the lady who took me in and raised me when my parents passed, died last night."

Tears began to escape the confines of Alexandra's long lashes, and her voice quivered over that word, *'died'*, it seemed so final and harsh as it left her lips. Alexandra tried to hide her face with her free hand, embarrassed by the sudden outpouring of emotions, her lips quivered as she gulped in air between sobs like a small child's heartbroken cry. Devastation was clear in every breath. Casey gently took the mug from Alexandra's shaking hand and placed it on the table. Then, like it was the most natural and comfortable action in the world, as if they had known one another for their whole lives, Casey wrapped her arms around Alexandra, cradling her. Neither of them said a word, Casey just stroked Alexandra's hair out of her face and held her gently as she cried.

The rest of the day had been a blur after that. Alexandra remembered Casey leaving for work, and her offer for Alexandra to call her anytime. She remembered packing her clothes into her beat-up case. She could recall Micah arriving to pick her up in his dusty old truck, and pulling into the station. But the whole day seemed to have taken place in silence, like she was trapped in a different world to everyone else. She could hear and see the world around her, but an invisible barrier separated her, like a protective bubble trying to keep her safe. Or was it keeping everyone else safe from her grief? Either way, she felt disconnected and alone.

[Present day]

"Tickets! Tickets, please!" boomed a loud voice down the train carriage, startling Alexandra out of her reverie. A tall, thin gentleman with a dark and out-of-place moustache stopped at her seat looking expectantly at Alexandra.

"Tickets, please?"

Luckily, that was the only human interaction Alexandra had to endure for the entire journey. She wasn't sure if she could cope with feigning politeness for more than the few minutes it took to show the conductor her ticket.

Alexandra faded in and out of restless sleep as the train chugged along. She was awoken fully only once during the six hour journey, by the tannoy announcing her arrival at Kingston station.

The distinct yellow walls and grey skies were not as welcoming as they used to be. Alexandra fought her way from the platform to the taxi rank, dragging her reluctant suitcase behind her. The sound of Christmas tunes, that Alexandra would usually be happy to hear, felt out of place and wrong to her today. The same baubles and lights, that were here each year as soon as it hit December 1st, decorated the station. Alexandra kept her head down and trudged towards the exit. Her Christmas spirit was in tatters and she was not sure it could fixed.

Alexandra was relieved to find a free taxi idling at the curb. With no queue in sight, she made a beeline straight for it, dumping her case in the trunk the second the driver popped it open.

After a few wrong turns and a taxi ride that had Alexandra thinking she might be joining her Aunt Alondra in the 'great beyond', the yellow cab took a sharp turn onto the dirt driveway leading to Chadwick Manor. (Alexandra slammed into the side door, the driver oblivious to the rollercoaster ride she was experiencing in the backseat.) The house loomed at the end of the road, its red brick turrets and large grey roof usually dominant in the centre of the vast fields of green surrounding it. But today, the snow-covered landscape and ice-covered roof made the manor seem smaller. Like it too, was grieving and disconnected from the world.

The Cosantóirí

It felt so strange to be back home; it had been so long since she had ventured back to the so-called 'Ocean State'. From the moment she received her acceptance letter into Berkeley, Alexandra had barely looked back. And when she graduated with a degree in Architecture, she had moved to Baltimore for a job. Close enough to visit if she had the urge, but far enough away that no-one reacted with pity or fear when she announced her last name was Chadwick.

Alexandra had never understood what made the Newport locals so apprehensive about her, her name, or her family. As far as Alexandra could tell, the family had lived in Rhode Island for centuries with no bother. Until the night Alexandra had been told her parents had died, nothing especially dramatic had happened to the Chadwick's.

The taxi came to idle alongside the manor, and the driver opened the door with a triumphant smile as if he too was impressed they had survived the journey. Wyatt was waiting for her atop the steps of the entryway, like he always was when she came home. His salt and pepper hair was tamed into a quiff of sorts, and he was donning one of his familiar plaid shirts - this one in a striking red. Since the day Alexandra had come to live with Aunt Alondra, Wyatt had become both her best friend and her baby sitter, her unexpected sounding board and her go-to for advice. Wyatt was the Chadwick's housekeeper in title, but in reality, he was family. Alexandra dragged her suitcase along the overgrown grassy path, slipping and sliding on patches of ice and snow as she went.

"Miss Alex. Please, let me assist you with your bags," Wyatt implored, making his way down the stairs to greet her. His soft British accent always made him sound concerned, but polite.

"It's okay Wyatt, I've got it." Alexandra responded stubbornly.

Alexandra had never liked other people doing things for her. Even as a small child she had always felt it was important that she knew how to take care of herself. Maybe she had always been planning for this day, the day when she was the last living Chadwick, without even realising it.

*****

The moon glowed bright and determined in the sky as Alexandra sat on the porch wrapped in a warm blanket. The glowing embers in the fire pit kept the icy chill of the winter air at bay. It had been two days since she had returned home, and still she could not sleep.

"You and I seem to be sharing a similar sleeping pattern" she mused out loud to the moon.

The moonlight was so vivid she could still see the snowy ground around her. She could pick out the icy trees wilting under the weight of the winter and the letterbox that, in the summer, marked the line between grassy yard and gravel driveway. The letterbox. Alexandra's eyes locked onto the box, taking in the gold script that read *Chadwick Manor*, as she noticed its door slightly ajar. She could have sworn that no post had been delivered since she had arrived. In fact, she would have bet money on it. But, as she rose stiffly from the comfort and warmth of the porch chair and made her way closer to the letterbox, she could see the corner of an envelope protruding from the metallic box before her.

Cold, wet snow was seeping through the fluffy slippers on Alexandra's feet by the time she was close enough to retrieve the letter. Her breath was visible and her lips tinged blue as she wrestled with the stiff letterbox that held on tightly to the crisp paper envelope. Aunt Alondra's messy scrawl was instantly recognisable the moment the letterbox gave in and handed over the goods. Alexandra had seen that scrawl in every birthday card, every inspirational post-it note in her lunchbox, every gentle reminder on the notice board. But this was no inspirational post-it or reminder to empty the trash. This scrawl simply read *Alexandra*. A rustle in the trees sent shivers down Alexandra's spine as she realised she could no longer feel her feet. Like lifting lead weights, Alexandra lifted her now sopping-wet slippers one at a time and as fast as she could until she reached the foyer of the manor. The heat of the house burned as her skin thawed, life returning begrudgingly to her toes as she kicked off her fluffy ice blocks and swapped them for warm dry socks. Alexandra shuffled the short distance from the foyer to the kitchen, shaking flecks of ice from her curls. (The duck egg blue walls and light wood worktops, although calming, were a stark contrast to the rest of the house.)

The rest of the house had been left in the Victorian era, whilst the kitchen had been yanked into the 21st century against its will. Alexandra dropped the letter on the breakfast bar, suddenly opening an envelope seemed to be the most challenging act in the world.

"This is going to require alcohol" she muttered to herself. "Lots of alcohol".

Alexandra grabbed a selection of ciders from the fridge. Aunt Alondra had a thing for ciders of the world, so her collection was always impressive. Alexandra had gone for her favourites; the bright yellow label of a fizzy English cider, a fruity one from some obscure French village, and one from Ireland (chosen for its alcohol content and not its taste).

Popping the top off of the first cider bottle and taking a swig for courage, she sat and stared at the envelope before her. She turned it over and over with her fingertips for a while, feeling its weight - unnaturally heavy for such a small envelope.

Finally, Alexandra levered the flap of the envelope open. Something small but solid sat inside, along with some folded paper. Alexandra tilted the envelope and watched as a rusty gold key clattered onto the worktop. Reaching across the work surface Alexandra retrieved the key, turning it over in her palm with confusion. A thin silver chain was attached to the key, and it glittered unnaturally in the light of the room, making the rusted key look even older than it had before.

Focusing on the strangeness of the key was helping Alexandra, helping her to procrastinate and avoid having to read the letter. She didn't want to read any final words, any last wishes, or sage words of advice from beyond the grave. Reading the last scrawl lovingly etched out by Aunt Alondra would truly mean she was gone, that she was never going to burst through the front door exuberant and full of laughter… It would be final. As final as the word itself, she would be dead. It sounded silly even to her own tired and buzzed brain. Aunt Alondra had died three days ago, and her funeral was in the morning. That was as final as it got. Alexandra delicately slid the paper from the confines of the envelope, the hot sting of tears behind her eyes as she began to read.

My Dearest Alexandra,

There is much I have not told you, and for that I hope you can forgive me. It was both mine, and your parents' wishes that we protect you for as long as we could. But if you are reading this letter, then the day has come when I can no longer shield you from what is to come.

I need you to know that I love you, and that I am so sorry for the burden that will befall you at my passing. I do not have the time left to tell you all you need to know, except that the key before you must be kept close to you always. It is your way home.

What you will discover in the days to come may seem overwhelming; it was for me at first too, but Wyatt is there to help you. He can answer your questions, but for the most part you will have to trust that the answers will find you when you need them most.

Love Always,
Aunt Alondra

Tears hurtled down Alexandra's cheeks, dropping on to the breakfast bar. She could not pinpoint how to feel. Alexandra was angry and confused, sad and heartbroken, and overwhelmingly lost. As last words went, and Alexandra had not been privy to many last words (but perhaps more than some,) they were devastatingly unclear in their finality. The words left more questions than answers, and with no author to answer them.

CHAPTER 2

THIS WOULD BE THE second funeral Alexandra had attended, but the first she would remember in full. She had been young before, when her parents had died, she hadn't fully understood. Not that she was sure she understood now either. But, the memories of her parents' funeral were hazy snippets, like poorly printed Polaroids in her brain. What stood out most - whenever she tried to remember - were the feelings of dread and fear that filled her.

Since that day, she had experienced those same feelings whenever she entered a church. Alexandra had never been overly religious; she believed in something sure, in magic, in kindness, in faith of some kind, but not necessarily in an almighty being. The fact that the church scared her and made her uncomfortable probably didn't help. It's hard to find peace in something that makes every fibre of your being want to run in the opposite direction.

Aunt Alondra's funeral was to have no church service -unlike Alexandra's parents' funeral - just a graveside service would be held. It was what Aunt Alondra had requested, and selfishly Alexandra was grateful for that. Grateful to not have to step into the same church where she had said goodbye to her family, to her childhood. Aunt Alondra's other request was somewhat more untraditional. Bright coloured hats. Alexandra had burst out laughing when the notary had revealed this little titbit of information.

Bright coloured hats. Of all the requests, Alexandra had thought, Aunt Alondra chose bright coloured hats. Alexandra's laughter was cut off by a twinge of pain in her heart, a twinge of grief at never getting to be a part of Aunt Alondra's quirky schemes and fun requests again. After today Aunt Alondra's wild and beautiful character was no longer going to be there to brighten up Alexandra's days. But for today… Bright coloured hats.

Alexandra had not had time to shop for a hat, or a dress for that matter. She had been so busy arranging the funeral and trying to wrangle her emotions in preparation to hear the words *'sorry for your loss'* from every attendee, that it had slipped her mind. So that morning, jumping awake from the buzz of the alarm, Alexandra was surprised to find a bright orange hat -her favourite colour- and an elegant black suit laid out on the end of the bed waiting for her. The blazer had a collar made of black velvet, subtle in its beauty against the crisp black of the rest of the suit. Next she inspected the orange chiffon hat, with its delicate swirling flowers, and its dainty size. It would sit nicely with her dark curls she thought.

"Wyatt, you're a star." Alexandra whispered to the empty room.

Wyatt's fashion sense was surprisingly exquisite. He had basically been her fashion guru through high school, probably saving her from many a fashion faux pas. The suit fit perfectly, as she knew it would; after all, Wyatt was practically an expert by now. Looking in the full length-mirror encased in an ornate gold frame, Alexandra placed the sunny orange hat atop her now glossy and tamed curls. The glint of something shiny caught her eye from across the room. She turned, curious. It was the key. Alexandra had almost forgotten all about it. She took a few strides towards the desk where it lay, looking at the strange glimmering chain and its decrepit key. Still none the wiser as to why Aunt Alondra had left this to her, Alexandra collected the key and hearing Aunt Alondra's words '*the key before you must be kept close to you always, it is your way home,*' Alexandra placed the cold chain around her neck.

As the key touched her skin Alexandra could feel a soft, slow vibration and a delicate humming emanating from it. She lifted the key to her ear, but nothing; the room was silent once again. Alexandra shook her head, slightly concerned that sleep deprivation was turning her crazy.

"I guess it's slightly more original than a locket or a ring for an heirloom."

Alexandra pondered as she tucked the key beneath her blouse and headed downstairs towards the foyer. Wyatt was waiting by the front door to usher Alexandra outside, down the driveway, and into the black town car.

*****

Pulling up to the cemetery Alexandra was taken aback by the sea of colourful hats spread amongst the gravestones. A slight smile appeared on Alexandra's face, tears in her eyes and her voice catching slightly as she spoke.

"Look at all these people, Wyatt."

"Alondra was very loved, Alexandra," Wyatt responded, his voice shaking with emotion.

"She really was," Alexandra replied, reaching forwards from the back seat to place a comforting hand on Wyatt's shoulder. He patted her hand delicately with his own, clearly appreciative of the daughterly gesture.

Wyatt cleared his throat and took a steadying breath.

"Are you ready, Miss Alex?" he asked.

"Aunt Alondra needs me to be ready," said Alexandra. Wyatt nodded in response as he opened the car door. Alexandra followed suit, leaving the safety of the warm car for the ocean of rainbow hats. As Alexandra made her way across the cemetery, careful not to walk across the final resting places of others, she could feel eyes following her as she moved. The pool of hats was suddenly aware of her presence, and they had all turned their attentions on her. If Lady Liberty and Christ the Redeemer where human, Alexandra imagined that this was how they would have felt - ogled and uncomfortable. Nevertheless she persisted, forwards towards the plot where Aunt Alondra was to take her final bow, adored by an audience of brightly coloured hats.

The ceremony passed by in an instant, so quickly that Alexandra could barely remember the event. People spoke, people laid flowers, people cried. She cried, she spoke, she cried again. Those were about all the details Alexandra could piece together as she stood staring at the coffin in the ground, the sea of hats returning from where they came. Alexandra was so lost in her own thoughts she barely noticed the man standing beside her.

"I am so very sorry for your loss, Miss Chadwick." the man said with a Spanish lilt to his words. "No one is ever ready for these things," he stated before walking away.

Alexandra turned to answer him, but the man was already a fair distance away. He was surprisingly spritely for a man who looked to be in his sixties.

"Hector?" shouted another woman Alexandra did not recognise. She had an accent too, European of some kind, but not one Alexandra could exactly place. Alexandra watched them walk a little while longer, before returning to her thoughts, the interaction with Hector pushed to the back of her mind. Alexandra had more important events to process.

*****

Alexandra writhed around in her sleep as she tried to push away the snapshots flashing into the foreground of her dream world. 11-year-old Alexandra stood in the foyer of the Chadwick Manor, her parents pale and motionless on the floor before her. Blood pooled on the wooden floor and decorated the walls. A loud crash echoed around the house as Aunt Alondra screamed for Alexandra to hide. Flashes of faces, some she recognised and others she did not, popped in and out of her mind.

A crash startled Alexandra awake. Her eyes opened as she launched from the bed, searching the room wildly for the source of the noise. The loud crash again. Alexandra swivelled on the spot, raising the alarm clock in her hand ready to strike, but this time she watched as the window swung wide and then crashed back against the frame. *It is just the wind,* she told herself, breathing a sigh of relief, as she reached over to latch the window closed.

Leaning against the windowsill she could feel the beads of sweat clinging to her skin and the tear tracks that had stained her face. Alexandra placed her weapon back in its rightful spot by her bedside, an exasperated chuckle escaping her lips at the thought of using the tiny alarm clock to wade off intruders. Alexandra shivered and reached for her Berkeley hoodie, confused by the vivid pictures from her dream.

They had seemed more real than a dream, more like memories. But that couldn't be, she thought, she was at a sleepover the night her parents died. Alexandra looked back to the alarm clock; it read 05:11am. Certain she would not fall back to sleep Alexandra dug a book out of her bag, chucked on a pair of comfy jeans, and curled up in the reading chair on the other side of the room.

"She needs more time to grieve. Miss Alex is not ready for all of this, not yet," the pleading in Wyatt's voice carried from the foyer to Alexandra's room.

The desperation broke through Alexandra's consciousness, making her stir. She must have nodded off, the book still open on the same page in her lap, but the alarm clock now reading 08:37 am. Alexandra craned her neck trying to hear the second voice, but both were barely audible from this distance. Alexandra quietly closed her copy of *Women Who Run with the Wolves*, slipped her feet into some comfy daps, and crept out onto the landing. Avoiding the creaky floorboards, (which felt like muscle memory she had done this so often,) Alexandra edged along the corridor to the top of the winding staircase. From here she would be hidden from view, but

21

able to hear everything. This had been her route to sneak into the kitchen for cookies at night, or to eavesdrop on Aunt Alondra and her gaggle of quirky friends.

"The Cosantóirí needs her to be ready now. We have waited longer than usual, out of respect for Alondra."

Each word the stranger spoke was bathed in a thick Spanish accent. His tone was calm, but authoritative. The man's voice sounded oddly familiar to Alexandra.

'Cosantóirí' Alexandra whispered to herself. Struggling over the foreignness of the word.

"You know as well as I do how dangerous it is to keep her in the dark, Wyatt. For Alexandra, and for the others too," the stranger continued in a hushed tone. "When Alondra passed, God rest her soul, Alexandra became the new protector of the Chadwick Tairseach. Whilst we wait, the Tairseach is vulnerable. I don't think I need to remind you of what happens when someone decides to take advantage of that vulnerability. Do I?".

Wyatt sounded defeated when he finally replied.

"No. A reminder is not necessary, Hector. But Miss Alexandra is not ready."

"No one is ever ready for these things." The man retorted.

Alexandra flashed back to Aunt Alondra's funeral. The man at the graveside, he had said those same words. She racked her brain trying to remember. Hector. That was what the European woman had called him. This was definitely the same man. A wave of nausea and stress hit Alexandra like a baseball to the face, stunning her.

Disoriented and confused, Alexandra slid slowly down the wall until she sat in a heap on the floor. Her brain struggled to process everything she had overheard.

What had she overheard? What in the hell was a Tairseach? Who did this Hector think he was, and what on earth made him think she could protect anything? *I can barely keep a plant alive, even cacti struggle to thrive under my care,* thought Alexandra with panic. The sound of something vibrating, loudly, interrupted her meltdown.

"Crap!" Alexandra exclaimed. Her phone had slid from her pocket and was edging its way across the floorboards with every buzz. There were no voices downstairs, just silence, then the familiar creak of the stairs and Wyatt's heavy footsteps getting closer. Alexandra retrieved her phone, silencing it in the process, but the damage was done.

"Miss Alex! What are you doing?" Wyatt asked, taken aback by Alexandra's presence on the floor.

Alexandra realised how strange she must look. On her hands and knees crawling along the landing with her phone in one hand.

"I dropped my phone." she responded weakly.

As soon as the words left her lips Alexandra could feel the poorly crafted lie, and the response on Wyatt's face told her that he too could feel it.

"You dropped your phone? Out here, in the hallway?" a smug grin played at the corner of Wyatt's mouth.

"Uh huh. Yep. It just fell right out of my pocket. Right here. In the hallway." Alexandra floundered.

Wyatt's smirk widened. "And what exactly are you doing out here, in the hallway?" he asked with glee.

"Just, you know, stretching my legs." replied Alexandra, her face blushed slightly, she knew the lies were weaved into a weak web.

"You have always been a terrible liar, Miss Alex." Wyatt responded, raising an eyebrow as if to emphasise his point.

"I will take that as a complement." Alexandra responded, trying hard to deflect.

"It was meant as such, Miss Alex." said Wyatt. "Am I to assume that you have been out here for a while Miss Alex?"

"You know what they say about people who assume, Wyatt." Alexandra mocked.

Wyatt looked unimpressed, "Hmmm, indeed I do." he replied.

Wyatt's face paled suddenly, like a ghost had passed by, or a sudden onset of illness had taken a hold of him. Alexandra was fairly certain neither had occurred in the last ten seconds. Wyatt's deep brown eyes were fixed on Alexandra. To be more specific, Alexandra realised he was staring at her neck.

"Do you know what that is?" Wyatt asked, concerned.

Self-consciously, Alexandra followed Wyatt's pointed stare down to the key, now freely dangling on the outside of her hoodie.

"A key?" she asked with uncertainty. "But to what, I don't have a clue. Though judging from your face, and the conversation you just had with Hector at the door, I'd bet *you* know." Alexandra's words came out harsh and cold, surprising her.

"And that would be a winning bet, Miss Alex." Wyatt was trying for jovial, but his voice was strained and tired-sounding.

"So what do I win?" asked Alexandra.

"The truth, Miss Alex. You win the truth." Wyatt replied.

Turning on his heels, signified by the slight squeak of his leather shoes, Wyatt began to head down the stairs. His greying hair looked dishevelled and longer than usual. The green plaid shirt Wyatt was wearing did little to disguise the stress that was clear in the lines of his scrawny shoulders.

"Wait! What truth?" said Alexandra, anger and frustration bubbling to the surface.

"Not here," Wyatt responded, his eyes still firmly forward as he descended the elaborate staircase. "Come," he gestured.

A mixture of curiosity and frustration propelled Alexandra down the stairs until she was almost on Wyatt's heels, both of them headed towards the kitchen. Just before they crossed the kitchen's threshold, Wyatt took a sharp right down another corridor. This hallway would lead them to the basement.

"Of course! The basement. The truth is always found in a dank, old basement." Alexandra exclaimed, sarcasm clear in every word.

Wyatt rolled his eyes slightly, but chose not to respond. To Alexandra's confusion, Wyatt stopped just shy of the basement door and stood staring at the obscure Salvador Dali hanging on the wall. Its ethereal style and imposing horse image had always seemed out of place compared to the rest of the paintings in the house.

"I feel like now is not the time to admire Aunt Alondra's eclectic taste in art, Wyatt," said Alexandra as she stood with her arms folded across her chest.

"I need you to be patient, not petulant, Miss Alex." Wyatt responded slightly exasperated.

"Excuse me..." Alexandra began to retort, but was cut off mid sentence by Wyatt removing the painting from the wall to reveal what looked like a small laptop screen.

Without saying a word Wyatt placed his palm onto the screen as a green light worked its way silently from palm to fingertip. Alexandra watched in disbelief, though she had to admit the nerd in her was completely freaking out at how Sci-Fi this was. Wyatt pulled his hand back, the screen now dark as if nothing had happened.

"Welcome Wyatt, portal guide to the Chadwick dynasty," echoed a robotic voice from the ceiling.

Alexandra flinched slightly, surprised by the sudden break from silence.

Wyatt turned to face Alexandra, his expression was not giving anything away. Instead he remained unnaturally stoic. "Your turn, Miss Alex."

Alexandra didn't know whether to laugh at the unexpected hilarity of it all, run in the opposite direction, or maybe check into an asylum of some sort. They all seemed like viable options. Instead, Alexandra lifted her hands to her face and slapped herself lightly on both cheeks repeatedly.

"What on earth are you doing?" Wyatt asked. "Just making sure I haven't accidently eaten one of Micah's homemade cookies again," replied Alexandra. She let her hands relax back at her side. "Do you hear that?" she asked.

A subtle humming filled Alexandra's ears, and the same slow vibration she had felt the day before began to emanate from the key around her neck. The sensation was both alien and yet oddly comforting at the same time.

Wyatt dodged her question. "Place your palm on the screen please, Miss Alex." he requested.

Alexandra took a step forward and positioned her hand at the centre of the screen. The green laser began its process from palm to tip, feeling warm on her skin. Then again the screen went black and Alexandra kept her hand there nervously.

"You can take your hand off now, Miss Alex." Wyatt whispered reassuringly.

"Welcome Alexandra Chadwick, descendant of the Chadwick Dynasty, defender of the Chadwick Tairseach, and member of the Cosantóirí." announced the computer.

Click, click, click.

The noise was coming from the floor behind Alexandra. Puzzled, she turned in time to see one of the large flagstones on the floor rising slowly with each *click*, hinged on one side to create a gap just big enough for one person to squeeze into. Alexandra took a step towards the ominous hole in the ground and a glint of silver reflected back at her. A steel ladder led straight down into the depths of darkness to whatever was there to surprise Alexandra next.

"Would you like to go first, Miss Alex?" Wyatt inquired.

"By this stage I feel like there is very little point in me saying no." Alexandra muttered as she walked towards the black hole. "I really hope there are no snakes, or anything else that bites, waiting for me at the bottom." she joked half heartedly.

"Don't worry, I will throw down your fedora and bullwhip when you reach the bottom." Wyatt grinned.

As Alexandra placed her feet carefully on the first rung, she could feel her daps slipping slightly on the cold metal, but she persevered, lowering herself down into the darkness.

"I don't think a fedora would fit down this hatch." responded Alexandra.

The journey down was cold, getting ever darker as she moved away from the light above.

"How long is this ladder?" she bellowed, her voice echoing back to her.

Wyatt offered no response. Either he had run off, and this was an elaborate prank, or she had descended so far down Wyatt could no longer hear her. Alexandra hoped for door number one, but was more certain that she had bulldozed through door number two.

"Great!" Alexandra sighed to herself, "I can't even see my feet anymore it's so dark down here."

As if Salvador Dali 2.0 - as Alexandra had decided to refer to the laptop in the wall - was listening, tiny green lights began to appear on either side of Alexandra. She could feel the light on her face, it's green glow bleaching the colour from her skin and revealing that the ground below was only a few rungs away. Dust rose in a cloud around Alexandra as she hopped from the last step of the ladder.

"Clearly this path is used often," Alexandra mocked, waving the dust away from her face. "But no snakes, I see," she whispered.

The clunk of boots against metal told Alexandra that Wyatt was on his way down to join her, and that he had indeed not run off and left her. Alexandra turned around slowly, taking in the concrete walls before her, the ebbing chartreuse glow adding an otherworldly aura to the new found tunnel under the Chadwick Manor.

Her curiosity well and truly peaked, Alexandra began to follow the tunnel until she reached a metal door. The sheet metal door took up most of the end wall, imposing and cold alongside the breezeblock walls. The only colour in the tunnel came from the glowing lights. Focusing on the centre of the metal door, Alexandra noticed a deep burgundy insignia, circular in shape and adorned with a single delicate gold feather. It stood out bold and bright amongst all the grey and metallic surroundings. The golden feather looked as if it had landed mid-fall from the heavens, sitting at a curved angle on its side. Alexandra reached out and touched the intricate gold lettering beneath the feather. It simply read *Chadwick*. Then a searing heat ran through Alexandra's body. Starting at her hand and coursing up her arm, it travelled to her heart and finished at her feet. She stumbled back, collapsing onto the cold hard ground as she fought to take in air.

The shock of the heat had winded her, and she was sure the smell of burning filled the air. Alexandra inspected her hand for trauma, but there was no mark to be found. Still struggling to control her breathing, Alexandra gazed back at the crest where fresh gold lettering had appeared, burnt into the burgundy. The source of the burning smell revealed, Alexandra rose shakily to her feet. She stepped forward towards the door, making sure to be close enough to read the new writing but far enough away to not get zapped again. The fresh gold ribbons had formed a new word before Chadwick, now the crest read *Alexandra Chadwick*.

Alexandra turned to run, this was one freaky Sci-Fi step too far even for her inner nerd, but she smacked straight into something solid. Panic was rising and clouding her vision.

"Miss Alex!" exclaimed Wyatt.

Alexandra realised she had run smack bang into Wyatt who looked taken aback and harassed. Alexandra's vision began to return to clarity as she distantly realised she probably looked like a wild animal caught in a trap all squirrely and wide-eyed. She sucked in a deep breath, and then another, trying to calm her fight-or-flight response.

"I see you touched the seal." Wyatt stated, staring pointedly at the fresh gold cursive.

"Are we witches?" Alexandra asked in a hushed voice. Wyatt laughed at this, and his face cracked into a giant smile. "It's not funny!" scolded Alexandra. "That thing burnt me, and my name just appeared out of thin air! Like...like magic".

"No. We are not witches, Miss Alex." Wyatt finally answered after his laughter shakes had subsided. "Though we do guard something equally as important as magic," he said. "We are guardians of a portal known as a Tairseach. This portal can take you to any place on Earth that you ask to go, so long as you have the key."

Wyatt pointed to the key at Alexandra's neck, which was still quietly humming with excitement.

Alexandra looked down at the still vibrating key, her mind swirling with confusion, a hint of excitement, and a dressing of disbelief.

"Wyatt, please don't joke with me right now. Is this for real?" she asked, vulnerability clear in her voice.

Wyatt placed his palm on the burgundy seal turning it clockwise.

"Yes, Miss Alex. This is all very real."

A delicate click sounded as Wyatt took his hand away from the seal, having twisted it ninety degrees. The door sunk back a few inches into the room behind it, and slid slowly to the left. The sound of metal against concrete made the ceiling shake, and the walls groaned in protest. The door continued to rumble sideways until the entryway was unobstructed. Wyatt flung his arm out in an elaborate gesture, as if he had finished a magic trick and was revealing the final twist. *Was he waiting for a round of applause?* Alexandra thought. Wyatt waved his other hand, the one not outstretched in the doorway, ushering Alexandra over the threshold.

"You, Miss Alex, are the newest member of the Cosantóirí. Welcome to your inheritance" Wyatt goaded.

"Cosan... What?" said Alexandra dimly. Her feet felt oddly heavy as she stepped warily into the room beyond the magic door.

"Cosantóirí, Miss Alex. It is Irish for 'Protector.'" explained Wyatt, as he calmly followed her into the darkened room. "As the only living member of the Chadwick Dynasty, and the Chadwick family bloodline, you have inherited the role of protecting the Chadwick Tairseach," he continued.

Alexandra did not know whether to laugh or cry, to run far and fast or to embrace this scary and exciting path like the characters in her favourite TV shows. The sceptic in her still had not settled on believing that a portal could truly exist. Flames burst into life around the edges of the room, each ebbing flame leashed to its own sconce on the old brick walls. Alexandra could feel the warmth on her cheeks, the smell of candles in the air. The fire was glinting off of something gold in the far corner of the room. It was a door, not large and obtrusive, but subtle and hidden in the corner. Its ornate golden frame, slightly rusted in patches, like the dirt was trying to hide its magic from the world. But Alexandra could feel it; any scepticism she had had before vanished. The humming of the key was in time with her heartbeat and she could feel an unexplainable connection with the door. Now she could see the beauty in the old rusted key around her neck, she could feel it in the connection to its other half - the door.

"This is it, isn't it?" Alexandra asked already knowing the answer. "Are there other portals? You said I am a member, which implies others too?" enquired Alexandra, as she walked slowly towards the door in complete awe.

"Yes. There are seven other dynasties, eight including yours, and together each member makes up the Cosantóirí. Each dynasty protects their own Tairseach, making eight portals across the globe," Wyatt clarified, pointing to the door at the word Tairseach.

"You sound like you have explained this before, Wyatt." Alexandra stated, her eyes still fixed on the door with childish wonder.

"That's because I have, Miss Alex. I am what is known as a portal guide. Which means that every generation of the Chadwick Dynasty is assisted by a member of my family. I have been the Chadwick guide for three generations of Chadwicks; Your father, your Aunt Alondra, and now you." Wyatt explained carefully.

"I can feel it." said Alexandra. "The door. The Tairseach. It's like it is a part of me."

"It is in your blood, Miss Alex." Wyatt smiled.

"Is this why they all died?" Alexandra turned to look at Wyatt, his smile faded to sorrow. "Mum, Dad, and Aunt Alondra I mean. Is this what killed them? I don't mean the door per se, but their association with it?"

"That is not a question I can answer for you, Miss Alex. They are stories for another time." Wyatt looked sad as he responded. "Right now, we need to get you to the castle."

"We have a castle?!" Alexandra asked, both confused and excited at the prospect.

"Not exactly. We used to own a castle in Ireland, where all of this originated. But since that site was compromised at the end of the 1500's we had to relocate to Éan and Claw Castle. The Castle has been owned by the Cosantóirí since the 1600's. It is a base camp of sorts, a safe haven for its members if you will."

"So how do I get there? Wherever there is," said Alexandra.

"The castle sits in the Scottish Highlands" responded Wyatt. "As for the how, you have a Tairseach Miss Alex."

Wyatt gestured around the room proudly, smiling excitedly like this answered everything. Alexandra stared at him for a beat, then looked back at the door in the corner. The door did not look like it could transport her to the end of the driveway, let alone to Scotland. But then things were, clearly, not always what they seemed in the Chadwick Manor. Alexandra stepped tentatively forward towards the door. The key at her throat humming louder and vibrating faster as if it was excited to see its other half.

"How does it work?" she asked puzzled and intrigued.

"That is the key," said Wyatt unhelpfully, pointing at the key around her neck.

"Yes. I am aware of what a key is, Wyatt.　How does this door work?" Alexandra snapped. She felt slightly stupid asking how a door worked, that query had never been a sentence she thought would leave her lips.

"The key, is the key to using the door, Miss Alex. What I mean to say is, that the key holds all the power. It is how you travel from place to place. Yet it cannot work unless the Tairseach is whole. You must travel through the door to, essentially, recharge the key." explained Wyatt. "Just open the door, step through with the key, and ask it to take you to Éan and Claw Castle." he said simply.

"You make it sound like I'm not just about to go from Rhode Island to Scotland by stepping through a decrepit looking door." Alexandra retorted.

Wyatt smiled sheepishly, but didn't respond.

"So I just step through. I just step through. This is no big deal, just a girl stepping through a door to go to Scotland. Completely normal. Okay, here goes nothing." she said, trying to convince herself to take the plunge.

Alexandra reached for the door handle slowly, she turned the knob until it unlatched the door from the frame. Pulling the door open revealed an almost indescribable scene before her. A mass of swirling colours greeted her. As Alexandra focused closer, she noticed the colours connected to make up images of distorted faces, landscapes, and scenes all swimming around. At first she felt icy cold, her breath visible as she opened her mouth in awe, then a heat wave seemed to strike and her cheeks began to redden. Wyatt must have felt the temperature change too as he reassured her.

"Different places have different seasons, Miss Alex. Winter and Summer can appear one after the other in the portal.".

"How do I know it is going to take me to the right place? What if it drops me in the middle of the Atlantic ocean?" Alexandra asked nervously.

"I assure you, as long as you ask it to take you to Éan and Claw Castle, it will. You can think the request, or say it out loud. However you feel comfortable, Miss Alex." Wyatt answered reassuringly. "Plus, you know how to swim if not." he winked cheekily.

"Funny." Alexandra retorted sarcastically. "Also, 'comfortable' is not really a place I'm at right now, Wyatt. But they say you should do one thing every day that scares you. I don't know who *they* are, or if *they* ever thought portal travel would be on that list of things, but who knows." Alexandra joked.

Humour had always been Alexandra's defence mechanism; whenever she was afraid, sarcasm was her safety blanket. *A positive attitude can pull you through anything*, her Mum had always told her. Alexandra wasn't sure she fully believed it, but she had always clung to the advice anyway.

"Safe travels, Miss Alex." said Wyatt. As Alexandra stepped gingerly over the threshold, her outline slowly disappeared into the sea of faces, places, and times. Wyatt delicately closed the door behind Alexandra, bowing his head as the door clicked shut. Wyatt closed his eyes and sent a silent wish to the ether to keep Alexandra safe. He had watched that sweet girl grow, helped to raise her. She was like a daughter to him, and Wyatt could not bear the thought of anything happening to her. But this; this was the job.

CHAPTER 3

THE SECOND THAT ALEXANDRA stepped into the Tairseach, the colours came alive. She could hear voices each with a different accent or language, horses hooves on cobblestones, car wheels screeching on the tarmac, winds howling through the trees, water crashing to the ground, gunfire and screams, people crying and shouting, and the quiet chirp of a single bird. It was like her mind could barely keep up with the many worlds flying past her eyes; the different smells in the air, the tastes on her tongue, and the tingling on her skin.

"Éan and Claw Castle. Éan and Claw Castle. Éan and Claw Castle." Alexandra repeated over and over to herself, in a whisper, like a mantra.

She closed her eyes picturing the words, trying to block out the worlds around her and really focus on those four words.
"Éan and Claw Castle. Éan and Claw Castle."

Alexandra felt herself being pulled by a force of some kind, like she was being plucked from the sea of worlds and dumped somewhere else. Her knees hit something solid, hard, the pain making her eyes water.

As Alexandra landed there was a loud *thud*, followed by a chorus of crashes and clatters. Then, startled voices began to break through the ringing in Alexandra's ears. *Oh no!* she thought. *Where on Earth have I landed?*

Slowly, Alexandra opened her eyes, blinking a few times trying to adjust to the light. To her horror, Alexandra had landed in the centre of what looked like a banquet hall. She was knelt precariously on a long wooden table, cutlery and plates strewn across the floor, and the table cloth bunched up at her knees where she had clearly slid a little way down the table. Even more horrifying were the eight sets of eyes all staring curiously at her. Alexandra could feel the heat rising in her cheeks, and for a moment, she felt paralysed by fear and embarrassment.

"You must be the new Chadwick?" said an English accent to Alexandra's right.

Alexandra tilted her head to see who the voice belonged to. An olive skinned woman, about Alexandra's age, with blonde surfer hair stared back at her.

Alexandra felt like she had left her words in the Chadwick Manor, when all that came out of her mouth as she tried to speak was a barely audible, hoarse, croaky *Yes*. She cleared her throat and tried again.

"Yes. I'm a Chadwick." she managed to say this time.

Alexandra scanned the room, unsure of what to do next. She had little experience of entering a room via portal and becoming a table centrepiece.

"Don't look so worried," said a dark haired, pale young man, with the same bone structure and English accent as the woman sat next to him. He leaned in conspiratorially, energetic in his actions. "The first time I travelled by portal I didn't even make it inside the castle. Nope. Landed straight in the blasted river outside. So you know, in comparison, this was really a very elegant entrance," the man said grinning cheekily. "I'm Skyler. Of the Adelmo dynasty. And this here is my twin sister, Shura."

Skyler gestured to the olive blonde seated beside him, who rolled her eyes with disdain. Alexandra couldn't help thinking how opposite the twins seemed to be. One so pale and dark haired with the happy energy of a child, the other, sun kissed and golden with the aura of a bored teenager. The only thing they appeared to have in common were their striking green eyes. Skyler offered his hand to help Alexandra down from the table. Relieved at an appropriate exit strategy, Alexandra took his hand and shuffled off of the table planting her feet on the floor. Skyler released Alexandra's hand with a theatrical bow, she could already tell he enjoyed the role of innocent jester.

"Sorry about all of this." Alexandra said, pointing to the dishevelled table arrangements she had left in her wake.

She smiled meekly, her wild curls even wilder than usual as she turned to take in the room from this new viewpoint.

"You can sit next to me," said a sweet accented voice from across the table.

Alexandra followed the sound, making eye contact with a baby faced girl no older than sixteen. Her loosely fitted turquoise headscarf glistened in the light of the room, the hue complementing her beautiful dark skin. Her deep brown eyes were friendly and welcoming, and full of wonder.

"O -okay. Thank you," Alexandra replied.

She felt very much like a panda in an enclosure, with a room full of people staring and watching her every move as she made her way around the large mahogany table. The imposing piece of furniture was surrounded by tall backed chairs, each one embossed with a different intricate design and velvet seat cushions in the same shade of navy as the table runner. The table runner that Alexandra had just used as a landing runway.

Alexandra arrived at the offered chair, taking a closer look at the carvings in the wood, she recognised the pattern on the back of the chair. It was the delicate feather of the Chadwick insignia.

"It is the Chadwick chair, no?" the girl stated. "Such a pretty picture you have, with the feather." she continued with a smile so bright and genuine it made Alexandra smile too.

"Thank you." Alexandra replied.

"My name is Ismat Williams, of the Williams dynasty. But everyone calls me Izzy." the girl said dropping to a whisper so only Alexandra could hear her.

"SÍ. SÍ. Welcome, welcome, Alexandra." a man's voice bellowed across the room, his Spanish accent drew Alexandra's attention.

She raised her head locking eyes with the older gentleman at the head of the table. He was the same man with leathery skin, and white hair that she had met at Aunt Alondra's funeral. This time he wore small, silver-rimmed glasses, and was sporting a chin full of greying stubble.

"You were there," Alexandra blurted. "At my Aunt's funeral. You were there." she continued.

"Yes. I was, Alexandra." He looked sad at the memory. "I am sorry that I did not introduce myself then, but it did not feel like the right time. My apologies for the deception. I am Hector Sarkis, of the Sarkis dynasty." Hector bowed his head slightly in both a greeting and an apology.

"I feel we should get back to business, Hector. There will be time for all this pleasantry later." said the woman to Hectors right.

Her German accent was subtle, but present as she spoke. She wore a power suit, which Alexandra had to admit she was jealous of, and her hair was controlled into a neat, mousey brown bun atop her head. She had been there too, at the funeral, thought Alexandra to herself.

"Of course, of course, Lexi." Hector replied kindly, as if the interruption had not been rude. "Back to business. Now. If someone could remind me of where we left off?" he enquired of the table.

Alexandra zoned out as the others continued on with lively debates and heated discussions. She was still processing the last few days, but tried to nod at what she hoped were the right times in the group conversation. The walls around her were built of thick rock and slate, with portraits hanging on every surface. From the ceiling hung an elaborate chandelier, the light bulbs out of place in the old style fittings where candles once lived. As she looked around the room taking in the old architecture, Alexandra could feel someone staring at her from across the table, but when she looked up the man opposite looked away. He was sweating, and his hands were shaky. Alexandra watched as he shuffled uncomfortably in his seat as if he would rather be anywhere but here. She couldn't help but wonder who this stranger sat across from her was, and why of all things he looked more nervous than she did. Alexandra did not have to wonder for long as Hector shouted across the table to the man.

"Raimund! Are you paying attention my friend?".

"Oui. Of course Hector. I just have nothing to contribute," Raimund replied in a thick French accent.

The man still looked jittery, and a little pale. Maybe he was just ill thought Alexandra, nobody wants to sit and chat when they've got the flu.

"Of course you don't," Shura said snidely.

Raimund flashed her a sarcastic devilish grin, but said nothing.

"Sascha, my dear. Did you have anything to add on this topic? After all you are based in London at the moment," asked Hector.

"No, nothing. Nothing to add." Squeaked Sascha, like a terrified little mouse caught in a trap. Her brown bob hid her face as Sascha ducked her head with embarrassment.

"Very well," said Hector.

Izzy leant closer to Alexandra, her voice at a whisper. "Sascha is very shy. She does not like to speak in front of everyone." Izzy commented, trying to help Alexandra to understand.

"Malandra? Any questions, thoughts, concerns?" Hector implored.

"Yes I do have one question, Hector," said Malandra. Her soft Canadian accent a calming relief to the ears after the previous heated debates.

Alexandra, only half paying attention, subconsciously reached up to the key around her neck as if to check that she hadn't lost it. It felt weirdly comforting to feel the subtle pulsing of the key at her fingertips as she tried to keep up with the conversation. A battle she was quite sure she was losing. Her mind drifted to the thought of what the castle grounds must look like if the inside was this elaborate, when a loud *crack* echoed in Alexandra's ears, a gust of icy wind and swirling colours plucking her from the comfort of the velvet seat. All of a sudden she landed with a *plop* on something cold, soft, and wet.

Alexandra could feel the icy water seeping through her jeans as she realised she was no longer inside the castle, but instead sat in the snow on the edge of a lake, the castle far behind her.

"Holy crap!" Alexandra exclaimed.

The cold winds stealing the breath from her lungs, and the feeling from her face. The scenery would have been beautiful, she thought, if the snow wasn't freezing her to the spot. Alexandra stiffly clambered to her feet, stumbling in the snow as she tried to stand. Wrapping her exposed hands inside her sleeves and crossing her arms as a barrier against the gale force winds, Alexandra searched around for how she had gotten here, and more importantly how she would get back to the castle before she froze to death.

Crack! The loud sound echoed around the loch, making Alexandra jump. The air in front of her began to shimmer and change. Alexandra stumbled backwards, fearing the cold had already frozen the synapses in her brain. Then, the air returned to normal as Shura appeared, gracefully landing on her feet, sinking slightly in the snow as she stabilised herself.

"You know if you were bored you just had to say. I mean this was a bit extreme, A.C." Shura joked, raising her arms up and motioning at the snow storm surrounding them.

"Nobody calls me that." Alexandra replied through chattering teeth, slightly taken aback.

"That is your main concern right now? Okay. Well 'Alexandra' just takes too long to say. 'A.C' is much easier." Shura responded all matter-of-factly, without making eye contact.

She seemed distracted scanning the frozen lake, and the snow-capped mountains around them. "Let's get back inside before tomorrow's local newspaper reads *two girls freeze to death on castle grounds discussing nicknames*" she jested, using both of her hands to imitate the newspaper heading in the sky.

Shura stopped scanning her surroundings, turning to look at Alexandra, she had a half-cocked grin on her face. Shuras' green eyes were vibrant in the snow globe of white surrounding them both, and for a second, Alexandra was lost staring at their clarity. Until Shura clicked her fingers in Alexandra's face, snapping her from her reverie, and returning her to a level of annoyance that overwhelmed her fear level.

"Are you ready to head back to the castle, A.C?" Shura asked impatiently.

"Are you always this. This..." Alexandra asked, struggling to get her words out in frustration.

"This what?" interrupted Shura.

"This abrasive." Alexandra finished.

"It's a special skill of mine, or so my brother tells me often." Shura replied unconcerned. "You'll learn to love my charm eventually." she smirked holding her hand out to Alexandra.

"I'm sure." replied Alexandra unconvinced.

"Come on then, the warmth is calling." Shura continued impatiently, grabbing a hold of Alexandra's unoffered hand.

Crack!

The sound reverberated around the loch, the same sound that signalled an incoming portal arrival. Shura turned to follow the sound, squeezing Alexandra's hand tighter, concern clear on her sun kissed face. The same disturbance of air, that Alexandra noticed when Shura appeared, was present not far from them. A spark of light, subtle but there, shot through the pulsing air pocket. Before Alexandra knew what had happened she felt Shura's hand being yanked from her own, followed by a scream of pain so excruciating Alexandra could almost feel the pain too.

Alexandra turned to see Shura slumped on the ground, her face hidden from view. Blood was seeping and spreading into the snow, and sticking to Shura's messy blonde hair. Alexandra rushed forward without thinking, rolling Shura carefully onto her back, desperately trying to find the source of the blood. She found it. A purple and gold dagger was protruding from Shura's shoulder. The hilt buried deep from the force of its strike.

"Shura!" Alexandra screamed with panic. "Shura, can you hear me? Shura!" Alexandra slapped Shura's cheek lightly, watching with relief as Shura's eyes fluttered open.

Her face had turned grey, and her lips were tinged with blue. "Shura, I need you to tell me how to get us back." implored Alexandra.

"The key. It's the same way you got out here." said Shura weakly, grimacing in pain at the effort.

Alexandra's brain was in overdrive; she couldn't think, she didn't know what to do, she could barely breathe. Then she heard it. Aunt Alondra's voice saying *The key. It is your way home.* A switch in her mind clicked, the panic pushed to the side as she grabbed the key around her neck with one hand and Shura's hand with the other.

Crack!

The white snow was replaced by beautiful colours, warm winds whipped at Alexandra's dark curls, and for a second she felt calm and safe. Then the biting cold returned, snapping at her face and toes like a vicious animal. This time Alexandra saw the ground coming and she pushed her feet forward bracing for impact, holding on to Shura with a vice grip.

They hit icy ground and Alexandra knew that they hadn't quite made it inside. Alexandra and Shura had landed just outside the castle door. Wishing desperately to cash in on any good Karma she might have left, Alexandra hoisted Shura to her feet wrapping the limp girls arm around her shoulder. Alexandra half carried, half dragged Shura towards the giant oak door.

Then she heard it again, *Crack!* Followed by a loud *thud!* Something had buried itself in the wooden frame of the door, just inches away from Alexandra's head. She spared a second to see what it was, confirming her suspicions that it was another dagger. Alexandra pushed the door

46

hard, using all her might. She could feel splinters from the aged wood digging into the exposed skin on her palm and wrist. *Come on!*

Alexandra yelled at the stubborn door. She let out a scream of frustration as she pushed her whole body weight into the door. Finally it budged, creaking with the effort of moving. Clearly the door had not been used in quite some time Alexandra thought trying to keep her fear at bay. Alexandra managed to create a gap just big enough to push Shura through. She landed with an unhealthy sounding crunch, and an awful moan of pain. Shura shuffled uncomfortably along the corridor so that Alexandra could slide her way through the gap between the door and its frame.

Crack!

Alexandra launched herself through the gap like she was making an epic save in a world cup final. She slid across the cool concrete floor her body too cold to feel any pain. The sound of a third dagger making contact with the oak of the castle door made Alexandra clamber to her feet. She placed both hands firmly on the back of the door and pushed, her face became a grimace of effort and power as she forced the reluctant door closed with a duff snap. Resting her forehead on the rough oak Alexandra took a deep steadying breath, her lungs struggling to fill and her heartbeat echoing in her ears.

Alexandra couldn't tell if she was going to throw up, pass out, or just burst into tears. Though as she glanced sideways, looking at Shura's pale and panicked face, she knew none of those choices were an option right now. Alexandra was very aware that she had no idea how to get back to the main hall, and Shura was definitely not up for a long tour of the castle in order to find it.

"Help! Help us!" Alexandra yelled down the corridor.

She lifted her hoodie off over her head, forgetting she still had her baby blue elephant pyjama top on underneath, and held the scrunched up hoodie around the knife in Shura's shoulder to stem the bleeding.

"Nice elephant." Shura mocked, in a weak raspy voice.

She looked even paler than she had outside and she was starting to shiver. The tapping of footsteps at the far end of the corridor halted Alexandra's retort.

"Help! Down here!" Alexandra called out.

The footsteps sounded faster, and they were getting closer. A hint of relief washed over Alexandra at the appearance of Malandra and Skyler. Their faces dropped at the sight of Shura propped against the wall, pale and bloodied. Alexandra holding pressure around the dagger with all her might, and her hands and clothes soaked with Shura's blood.

"Shura!" Skyler cried out with dread.

He dropped to his knees beside Shura, carefully moving Alexandra out of the way to hold pressure on Shura's wound.

"I've got it, Alex." He said, not unkindly. His green eyes met Alexandra's, tears catching on his eyelashes.

Alexandra nodded in understanding, and she obediently moved her hands away, pulling herself to the wall opposite where she sat exhausted and overwhelmed.

"Shura, honey. Keep your eyes open for me. Good girl." Malandra said calmly.

Her voice was reassuring and confident as she inspected her patient. "We need to get her to the infirmary," she said to Skyler.

Skyler nodded, reaching down to place a hand under Shura's knees and the other at her back, he scooped her up in his arms delicately as if she was a breakable china doll.

"Carefully, Skyler. We don't want to jostle the knife." Malandra coached reassuringly.

Alexandra watched as Skyler moved fast and steady down the hallway. She felt dizzy and her skin was burning from the heat inside the castle. Her fingertips tingled, and her body was starting to ache all over. Alexandra could feel the bruises now that she was warming up, she felt like she had been hit by a truck and it made her wish for the numbness again.

"Come on, sweetie." Malandra said as she crouched down in front of Alexandra taking hold of Alexandra's hand and lifting her to a standing position. "We need to get you checked out too, Alexandra." she continued.

"It's not my blood." Mumbled Alexandra, her mouth struggling to form sentences through frozen lips.

"Come now." replied Malandra simply as she led Alexandra towards the infirmary.

By the time Alexandra and Malandra had entered the room, Skyler had already placed Shura on one of the patient beds and was frantically collecting up medical supplies. The infirmary was not at all what Alexandra had imagined, sure it had medical equipment, and beds with white linens, but the walls were the same stone as the rest of the castle, and the room was on basement level with no windows. If it hadn't have been for the modern machines and fancy medical tech, Alexandra would have thought she had returned to the dark ages. She looked around half expecting to find a mortar and pestle, and a counter full of herbal remedies. No such items appeared, to her relief.

"Sit." Malandra instructed softly, pointing Alexandra to the bed just down from Shura's. "Skyler, I need you to start an IV for me honey. You remember I taught you how to do that?" she continued.

Skyler nodded in answer, a response he maintained for each request Malandra threw at him. Alexandra watched as Malandra instructed Skyler to hand her different silver instruments from a tray table at the foot of the bed. She felt like she had used up an entire lifetimes supply of energy, and that she might never get it back. Her body was exhausted, but her mind was still racing as she watched Malandra pull the knife from Shura's shoulder; the splash of blood on the floor, Skyler's grave face, and then Malandra nodding triumphantly.

"There. The bleeding has stopped. She's all stitched up and almost ready to go." said Malandra with relief. "Skyler, why don't you go and get both the girls a change of clothes whilst I finish patching your sister up? Ask Izzy to help if need be, sweetie." she asked.

Though it was more of an order than a question. Skyler nodded, and without a word left the room running his fingers through his messy jet black hair as he went.

Malandra appeared in front of Alexandra, a basin of soapy water in hand, and she began to clean the blood from Alexandra's still shaking hands. Alexandra grimaced slightly as she realised some of the blood was her own. Splinters of wood were protruding from her arm and hand in various places. Malandra patiently removed each slither, gentle in her approach, wrapping Alexandra's hand in a soft clean white bandage when she was done. Alexandra had not noticed Skyler return with a change of clothes, but when she glanced to the side a stack of freshly laundered clothes sat at the foot of her bed.

"Why don't you get yourself cleaned up and out of these bloody jeans, honey. The bathroom is just behind you, to the left." Malandra instructed.

Alexandra nodded and made her way stiffly to the bathroom. She stared at her face in the mirror surprised to see a darkening bruise on her forehead and a graze on her cheek. Her skin was pink from the drastic temperature change inside the castle compared to the blizzard outside. Alexandra scraped her wild hair back into a messy ponytail pulling bits of dirt and debris out as she went. She splashed her face with warm water trying to remove the dirt and grime stuck to her skin. It took a while to remove the blood soaked jeans from her legs, the blood had dried slightly, making it stick to her skin through the denim. She finally freed herself and replaced the ruined jeans with the random pair of joggers Skyler had picked out for her. They were grey and warm, but far too big for her, though Alexandra was just grateful to not be clothed in somebody else's blood. Alexandra exchanged her pale blue elephant top for a much less gaudy black V-neck, and a burgundy zip-up jacket and made her way back to the Infirmary. The room was empty, apart from Shura resting peacefully on the only occupied bed. A little bit of colour had returned to Shura's cheeks and her lips were a more normal shade of pink. Alexandra pulled a chair up to sit at her bedside, she reached across to remove a clump of dirt from Shura's bedraggled hair, it's dirty blonde colour still tinged pink from the blood.

"You're definitely less abrasive when you're asleep." Alexandra mused, not expecting a response.

"I prefer the word charming to abrasive." Shura replied, her eyes still firmly shut but a sincere smile on her face.

Her voice was still weak, but the level of sass in Shura's tone suggested that she was feeling better already. Alexandra sat by Shura's bed, unsure of where she should be, or what she should be doing. She could feel her eyes getting heavier and heavier, and finally closing. Alexandra was grateful for the throws of slumber and the relief of a quiet dreamless sleep.

CHAPTER 4

A GENTLE TAP ON the shoulder had Alexandra jumping awake, startled and dazed. She blinked hard trying to focus, opening one eye then the other adjusting to the bright white light of the room. She was still perched on the stool at Shura's bedside.

"Sorry to wake you. But Hector would like to speak with you." Izzy spoke in a hushed tone, her face friendly and expectant.

"Sure. Sure." Alexandra responded whilst stifling a yawn.

"You've got a little, umm, something there." said Izzy pointing to Alexandra's face.

Alexandra reached up to her face wiping drool from her cheek vaguely mortified, but grateful for the honesty.

"Cheers. That could have been embarrassing." Alexandra jested sarcastically. Izzy blushed and bowed her head slightly, a childish grin playing at her lips.

"What time is it?" Alexandra asked, the lack of windows in the room not giving away any clues of whether it was day or night.

"It is the middle of the night, Alexandra. You have been asleep for a few hours." Izzy responded, still

53

speaking in a hushed voice. "Would you like me to show you to Hector?" Izzy enquired.

"That would be great. I'm bound to get lost otherwise." said Alexandra.

As they made their way to find Hector, Izzy walked several steps ahead of Alexandra bouncing along with unnatural excitement for the middle of the night. She was singing softly to herself in a language Alexandra could not understand.

"What language is that, Izzy? It sounds beautiful." Alexandra asked curiously.

"It is Egyptian Arabic." Izzy responded, turning to face Alexandra and continuing to skip backwards as she replied. "My mama taught me this song when I was small." she smiled at the memory then turned to face forwards again. "We are here." Izzy announced before Alexandra had time to respond to their previous conversation. "This is the library, where you will usually find Hector. He enjoys the many books, in many languages. I will leave you to speak with Hector."

Izzy inclined her head in a farewell gesture, and danced off down the corridor. Alexandra knocked reluctantly on the door, wishing she was curled up in her cosy bed in Baltimore.

"Come in." Hector instructed.

Alexandra unlatched the black iron door latch and eased the door open, it squeaked loudly as if it was not used very often. She didn't even notice Hector sat in the far corner of the room, Alexandra was too busy taking in the mountains of books all around her. There were stacks of books on every surface like book cairns in a field of yet more books. Alexandra plucked a green leather bound book from the top of the nearest cairn, its intricate silver lettering was so delicate and beautiful. She was surprised to find that the inscription read *Oliver Twist*.

"We have five copies of that book, each in a different language. It is so marvellous how stories can resonate across generations and geographical boundaries." Hector spoke from the corner of the room. He was sat comfortably in an antique looking leather arm chair. "You must have many questions, Alexandra." he stated.

"I don't even know where to start if I'm being honest. My mind hasn't caught up to my body yet, it's still stuck on the train in Baltimore I think." Alexandra replied.

She was distracted, still gazing around the shelves upon shelves of books. Some were beautifully intricate with old spines, and others were so shiny and pristine in their newness. Alexandra paused for a moment, collecting her thoughts, then she turned to look at Hector. His eyes were following her curiously as she perused the library's impressive collection.

"I guess my first question is, who threw the daggers? Or should it be where did the daggers come from? I'm pretty sure the two are one in the same." she supposed.

The more she thought about the last few days, the more Alexandra realised she did indeed have many unanswered questions, they were flying into her mind like a postal delivery of queries and concerns. As if they had been laying dormant whilst she flew through the Tairseach, whilst she ran from mysterious flying daggers, and whilst she watched as a girl she barely knew bled out on the floor of a castle she had never seen before. Her curious mind had awoken and she was ready for answers.

"In order to answer that question I first need to tell you more about our history. The context is important, Alexandra. Why don't you sit." said Hector offering her a seat in the chair opposite him.

Alexandra weaved her way through the book cairns and sat heavily in the cold leathery seat.

"I made us some tea, I heard you are also an Earl Grey fan." Hector continued, emptying the gaudy bird covered teapot into two cups. He placed the teapot back down on the small table between them. "Sugar?" he asked.

"One sugar. One milk." replied Alexandra, as if she was just meeting a sweet but secretive old uncle for tea. Hector smiled and slid a cup across the table to her.

"I do not know what you have been told already about the Cosantóirí, or if indeed you have been told anything. Normally we are much more formal about introducing new members into the fold. But I'm afraid special circumstances meant that we had to do things a little differently with you." said Hector as he stirred sugar into his tea.

"Special circumstances like daggers appearing out of thin air and almost killing people?" Alexandra enquired, a hint of sarcasm in her words.

"SÍ. That is one such example." Hector replied. "Let us start at the beginning, and hopefully many of your questions will have answers by the time I am finished." he smiled kindly.

Hector took a sip of tea, sitting back in his chair and settling in for the upcoming history lesson.

"The Cosantóirí was founded in 1580, after a group of smugglers discovered the first Tairseach. This group consisted of what we now refer to as the founding dynasty's. Gabe Garmund, Samuel Adelmo, Marcus Sarkis, Emily Eames, Dale Fremont, Charles Abernethy, Christopher Delmira, Timothy Williams, and Tavy Chadwick." Hector began, his demeanour showed that he enjoyed telling this tale. "The story goes, that during the Second Desmond Rebellion in Ireland, Tavy Chadwick and Samuel Adelmo mapped out underground tunnels in order to help innocents to escape the fighting in Limerick. These tunnels spanned from Limerick to Kerry, and on to Cork. But the tunnels were too long for just the two of them to maintain, so they enlisted the help of Marcus Sarkis, Emily Eames, Dale Fremont, Charles Abernethy, Christopher Delmira, Timothy Williams, and Gabe Garmund in order to keep the 158 kilometres of tunnel space safe. When Tavy and Samuel decided to expand the tunnel system, the others offered to help. During the first dig they came across a hidden bunker of sorts. Inside they found what we now call a Tairseach.

"Charles Abernethy was the first to go through the door, and he was transported to North Wales. The others assumed that Charles had died, and fearing the doors powers, they decided to move it to a safer location where they would study it and protect it. It was moved to the basement of Desmond Castle where it stayed until 1593." Hector paused to sip his tea, Alexandra followed suit awaiting the rest of the story.

"By 1588 the smugglers had learnt how the Tairseach worked, and were using it to transport people around Ireland. They called themselves the Cosantóirí - the

Protectors. In 1591 Gabe Garmund, a brilliantly smart man, discovered how to replicate the Tairseach and over the next two years he built seven more portals. One for each of the surviving founding members. He realised that the power of the Tairseach could be extended beyond the door using a key. The key would allow the user to harness the power of the Tairseach from a distance, but could not work alone," Hector continued.

"When Charles Abernethy returned in 1593, he demanded to be given the first Tairseach, after all he had been the first to step over its threshold. But the Cosantóirí refused. In the years that Charles had been gone he had built up an army. And in December of 1593, he marched that army into the castle grounds killing Dale Fremont, and Emily Eames. Most of the castle was destroyed and the rest of the Cosantóirí fled to Scotland, taking refuge in Éan and Claw Castle, transporting the Tairseach with them. They decided that it was too dangerous to keep all the Tairseach in one place so they divided the portals around the world. It was during this division, that Gabe gifted each member with a key that corresponded to their Tairseach. The Chadwick's moved to America, the Sarkis' to Cuba, the Garmund's to Germany, the Adelmo's to England, The William's to Egypt, and the Delmira's to France. The Fremont Tairseach was handed down to Dale's daughter, Delilah, who moved it to Canada. The Eames portal went to Emily's sister who moved it to Russia. Gabe Garmund refused to make any more Tairseach as he was worried that they could become weapons in the wrong hands. A fear he was right to have. Gabe destroyed most of his research, but some remained at Desmond Castle."

Hectors voice had taken on an ever more theatrical tone as he continued with the story.

"But that still doesn't explain who threw the daggers, and how." Alexandra prompted.

"Well. Over the years the Abernethy's have been trying to build their own Tairseach using what is left of Gabe's research. They had been unsuccessful, until now. A few months ago we found out that the current Abernethy heir had developed technology synonymous with the Tairseach. The current Abernethy, known only as 'Bas'- which is Irish for Death - has been using this technology to build their criminal organisation. They transport drugs, weapons and women all around the world. Law enforcement can't keep up, no one knows what Bas looks like, and even we are too far behind in figuring it out. If Bas is able to destroy the Tairseach, like they hope to, we would be unable to compete.

"When the Cosantóirí was founded, it was done so to protect people, and though the threats and the technology may have changed over the centuries, our purpose and goals have not. We are here to protect. We guard the Tairseach so that Bas cannot gain control of them, we protect the rest of the world from the knowledge that such science exists, and we protect anyone who falls victim to the misuse of Tairseach technology." Hector spoke with pride, his posture changing in sync. To answer your original question. The person who threw the dagger was Bas, and the how, unfortunately, is by using a technology that we don't fully understand." Hector finished, placing his cup back on the table.

"How come they didn't follow us into the castle? As soon as I shut the door, the daggers stopped flying." asked Alexandra. She was sat on the edge of her seat, leaning forward eager to know more.

"When the original Cosantóirí fled here in 1593 they placed protections on the castle. As far as we have been able to decipher, the protections emit an intricate combination of portal frequencies. These frequencies are able to match with the frequencies that each of our keys run on." Hector held up his key to clarify. "Each dynasty has its own specific frequency that connects them to their Tairseach and their key. When the Abernethy's were shunned, the intricate mix of frequencies was altered so they would be unable to enter the castle. The castle cannot be entered without a connection to these frequencies ." explained Hector. "Meaning that anyone with a bloodline connection to the Abernethy dynasty should be unable to step foot inside the castle."

"Well thank you, grandpa Tavy and gang for that, at least." said Alexandra dryly.

"SÍ. Thank you indeed." Hector agreed with a nod.

"The protections, on the castle, are they on our homes too?" enquired Alexandra hopefully.

"Unfortunately no, here is the only place the original Cosantóirí placed the so called 'portal pocket'. Theoretically we should be able to create more portal pockets to protect ourselves, but that knowledge was lost a long time ago." replied Hector.

Alexandra's face dropped, and she looked sad as she spoke. "Hector, did Bas kill Aunt Alondra?" she asked.

Hector was quiet for a moment as he considered his response. "We suspect that may be the case, but we do not know for sure, Alexandra." he replied. Hector looked away, avoiding eye contact with Alexandra, as if there was more to the story but he was not going to reveal it to her tonight.

"And my parents?" Alexandra probed, anger seeping into her words.

"Alexandra. You know how your parents died. There is nothing more I can add to that." Hector responded evasively.

"That is not an answer." Alexandra retorted, her voice rising in frustration.

A knock at the door interrupted the tense standoff taking place between Alexandra and Hector. Both of them locked in a staring contest of stubbornness. The door opened, and Hector broke from the contest, looking past Alexandra towards the doorway.

"Sorry to interrupt, but the others are getting restless. They want to know when they can return home?" Lexi's harsh tone was instantly recognisable as she spoke, Alexandra did not even need to turn around to confirm it.

"Ah, SÍ. The others. We are finished here. So..." said Hector.

"Are we? Finished?" Alexandra asked, cutting Hector off mid sentence.

"SÍ. For now, we are." Hector replied, his tone final. "Let us join the others. They are not used to being away from their posts for so long." he continued in a lighter tone, heading for the doorway as he spoke.

After a short pause, Alexandra followed Hector and Lexi down a maze of corridors back to the main hall certain she would never be able to retrace their steps. As they entered the room Alexandra noticed that the table had been cleared, but the smell of roast potatoes and gravy still filled the air. The smell made her stomach twinge with hunger, and she realised it had been a long while since she had eaten a full meal. Everyone was back in the main hall, even Shura who looked tired, her usual olive glow missing, as she propped herself up against her brothers shoulder, whose face was set in an unreadable expression. Izzy was fast asleep across two chairs, covered with a red woollen blanket, whilst Malandra and Sascha whispered in hushed tones to one another beside her.

Alexandra was always impressed by people who could sleep anywhere at any time, it had never been a strong skill set of hers. In the far corner Raimund was pacing back and forth, looking even more uncomfortable than the last time Alexandra had seen him. Lexi strode confidently over to where Izzy lay, reaching down she placed a hand on Izzy's shoulder and shook her gently until she woke.

"I know it has been a very long night for you all, and I thank you all for staying." Hector started. "The events in the past twenty-four hours have brought to light the very real threat that Bas poses to us all. So, now more than ever, it is important that we look out for one another. I suggest that we instigate 'blue spruce' protocol until the threat has been contained," said Hector. His face was oddly stoic.

Alexandra turned to Shura, a perplexed look on her face. "What is the 'blue spruce' protocol?" she asked in a whisper.

"It's the Cosantóirí's version of a phone tree. Basically, we have to check-in every twelve hours to a central system in the castle. If we don't, the system picks

it up and sends an emergency message to all members."
replied Shura in a soft voice.

"Bas may be a formidable threat, and one not to be
underestimated, but we have something that makes us
more formidable. We have each other to fight for, to fight
with, and to fight beside. That being said, as always, stay
alert and stay safe as you return to your posts." he
continued, an air of pride and faith in his words.

He turned to look at the twins perched against the
wall beside him.

"Shura, I would like you to accompany Alexandra
back to the Chadwick Manor. I feel it would be beneficial
for the both of you." said Hector, leaving no room for
any questions or arguments.

"Okay." Shura replied simply.

Hector turned to look at Alexandra. "I am sorry.
Sorry that we need you to be ready far more quickly than
is fair, Alexandra."

"It is time, Hector. We all have lives to be getting
back to." said Lexi. "I wish you all good luck. And
welcome to the Cosantóirí, Alexandra." she smiled. A
smile that softened her face, surprising Alexandra at the
sincerity in her words.

"Sí, sí. Of course. Stay safe, and goodnight." Hector
responded, bowing his head in a farewell gesture.

Lexi reached up to the key around her neck and the
air began to ripple around her, like a droplet of water
hitting a puddle. The familiar *Crack*, then she was gone,
the air quiet and still once again. Alexandra watched as
the other's disappeared from the room, each of them
nodding in farewell as they went, leaving the main hall
empty except for Shura and herself.

"Are you ready, A.C.?" Shura inquired.

"I guess I have to be." Alexandra replied, reaching out to take hold of Shura's free hand.

"You know what they say, *fake it 'til you make it*." Shura smiled, unconcerned.

Alexandra held onto her key, and closed her eyes picturing the poinsettia at the centre of the Chadwick Manor foyer, its red flowers vibrant against the dark wood table it sat on.

Crack!

CHAPTER 5

Sascha's feet touched down gently on the soft faux fur rug, she could feel her joints aching with fatigue from the long night. She was not used to so much human interaction, and much preferred her own company. She had been that way since she was a child, always much more at home in her own imagination than trying to navigate the intricacies of the real world. The rain pelted the windows, bouncing off of every surface in little droplets as Sascha made her way to the kitchen.

"Demetri. Come on little man, it's food time." Sascha cooed. The soft padding of tiny paws sounded on the floor, and then on the worktops as Demetri launched onto the kitchen side purring with delight. The smoky grey cat looked at Sascha with its intense green eyes, his tail curling back and forth like a serpent begging for attention.

"How do you feel about watching ER reruns and getting takeaway tonight, Demetri?" Sascha asked the cat who purred in response. Demetri circled back and forth on the worktop meowing loudly for food. "Alright, alright. I know you only suffer my company for the food." Sascha joked stroking the cat from head to tail.

She retrieved a tin of tuna from the cupboard and lovingly decanted it into Demitri's bowl. The flicker of a red light on the answer machine caught Sascha's attention. The small screen read one message, as it flashed like a red beacon. Intrigued by the unlikelihood of someone leaving her a phone message, and expecting a wrong number, she pressed the play button.

Hi Sascha. It's Damon, we met the other day at the library. The one on Chancery Lane. I'm not sure if you remember me, you probably don't, but if you do. Well, I was hoping you would like to meet me for a meal or a drink. Just hit me back if you fancy it. Sorry, I can't believe I just said 'hit me back', nobody says that. But, yeah, call me. Okay, bye.

Sasha blushed slightly at the message, she did indeed remember the man. He had been about her height, with vibrant ginger hair, adorable freckles, and glasses. She had thought he was very handsome, and he had a kind smile too. Sascha went to pick up the phone, excited at the prospect of a date with someone equally as awkward as she felt. Then she paused, her nerves getting the better of her.

"What would I even say, Demetri?" Sascha asked the cat. "What if he doesn't pick up? I'm terrible at leaving messages. Besides what would I even wear to a date?" she fussed, talking herself out of returning the man's call. "Maybe I will call him later." she resolved. Even Demetri rolled his eyes, knowing that she would still be too anxious to call Damon back 'later'.

*****

The aroma of leftover isku dhex karis filled the room as Malandra dropped softly onto the green cotton couch. Her Mother's Somali recipes were Malandra's favourite, they instantly transported her back to her childhood. They helped her to imagine that half of her heritage, to recall stories of a land that she was yet to experience. Malandra's stomach rumbled in response to the smell of food. It felt like it had been days since her last meal, even though she knew it had only been a few hours. She placed the leftovers in the microwave, looking at the planner on the wall as she did so.

"Crap!" Malandra exclaimed. "I forgot I'm on nights for the next two days.".

She glanced at the clock on the wall, realising she had two hours to get ready and into work. Malandra rushed around the house shoving items into her work bag, hastily changing into clean clothes, and taming her hair into some form of bun. The *ping* of the microwave echoed in the kitchen giving Malandra an excuse to sit for five minutes whilst she wolfed down the isku dhex karis. It tasted just how she remembered. *Almost as good as my mother's*, she thought.

Malandra managed to make it into the hospital with five minutes to spare, just enough time to dump her stuff in a locker and meet her interns for rounds. She was usually excited to get new interns, their eyes full of wonder and their hearts still set on saving the world. It was refreshing and a nice reminder of why she started this journey to be a doctor. But new interns on a night shift was a different story, they weren't used to the sleep deprivation yet, which meant she would have to deal with exhausted, overworked, and emotionally unstable interns for a whole night shift. Malandra was already tired, and did not feel prepared for the always eventful night shift.

As predicted the small group of interns were a mixture of over caffeinated and sleep deprived. To Malandra's relief they were still eager to learn, which meant they might actually pull their weight tonight and not just mope around complaining about the awfulness of a night shift. They were covering the emergency room tonight, a stark difference to the paediatric ward were Malandra usually spent her time. But a good way of brushing up on adult anatomy she thought, trying to stay positive.

"Okay, you must be my interns for the night. Have any of you done a night shift before?" Malandra asked in her work voice. Her less friendly, more authoritative voice, reserved for interns and idiots. Only one hand raised out of the five interns before her. "Great. Name?" she continued.

"Sandy. Sandy Granger." the woman replied confidently.

"Sandy, you know the drill. So I will be looking to you to help your colleagues out if and when they need it. Okay?" Malandra asked, though it was more of a command than a question. The other woman just nodded, a look of superiority flashed across her face.

"All of you grab a chart, see patients, and any problems you ask our fabulous nurses or you come to me. Let's be smart, and remember we are a team tonight, so let's work together." Malandra said, aware she sounded like she was coaching a little league team and not speaking to future doctors.

To Malandra's surprise the interns were fantastic, not that she would tell them that to their faces, they still had to feel like they needed to impress her, it was tradition. The shift went remarkably well, with only a few emergent cases, and a couple of quirky cases.

When 9:00 a.m. rolled around the interns looked even more exhausted than when they had met the night before, and the look of relief was amusing as Malandra ushered them home for the day.

"Get some sleep. Same again tonight." Malandra called after them to a response of half-hearted waves, and a few grunts. Malandra decided to take her own advice, and head straight home to sleep. She certainly needed it, she was running on at least thirty six hours without sleep. Worried that she might be too tired to drive, Malandra figured portalling home was the safest bet, and the quickest. A *crack!* Followed by bright swirling colours, and then she dropped onto her bed. She didn't even get up to change, Malandra was too tired, instead she fell asleep almost as soon as she had landed.

*****

Raimund landed in the dank, rubbish filled alleyway just around the corner from his least favourite bistro. *Fairy Tale of New York* was blasting out of the back of a nearby pub, Raimund was already fed up of the festive season and all the Christmas tunes around. His trainers were damp from the oil slick puddle he had stepped into, but he didn't care. Raimund was in a rush, his nerves screaming and his muscles twitching. He rounded the corner avoiding people in the busy Parisian streets, the hum of traffic and talking swelled up around him. Raimund reached his usual spot, perching nervously on the wicker chair outside of the disreputable cafe. He rubbed his hands anxiously together, teetering back and forth, agitated and uneasy. Raimund knew it did not matter that he was late because Street always kept him waiting, it was as if Street enjoyed tormenting him. Raimund searched the crowd until he spotted the familiar blue hat and oaf like figure making his way through the crowd. Street was finally showing his face. Well not his whole face to be exact, Raimund had never actually made eye contact with this man, only Street's blue cap and chiselled chin were familiar to him. But what could you expect from the man who sells you drugs thought Raimund, angry at himself for falling back into this cycle again. He knew how disappointed his family would be with him, if they were still alive, he could feel the disappointment himself as an ache in his heart.

"You're late." stated Street his voice unnaturally deep. He always sounded like he spoke through a voice modulator Raimund thought to himself.

"If I'm late, then you are even later." Raimund replied trying to keep his tone neutral, but failing.

"If you are going to be rude little Rai then I can just leave. But if I do that, then there's no candy for you is there?" Street jabbed back.

Raimund hated the nickname, his brother Philippe had always called him *Little Rai* and it had stuck. Philippe had been two years older than Raimund, his friends had seemed cool at the time, and so Raimund would hang out with them. The downside, he learnt too late, was that he picked up their bad habits. Street had been Philippe's supplier, and when he died Raimund inherited that too. You would think losing a brother to a drug overdose would have scared him straight, but Raimund was too stubborn for that. Raimund scolded himself internally, and held in his anger. After all he did need a fix, and Street was the only one who could give him what he needed.

*****

The comforting, clean scent of Lexi's home office welcomed her as she landed gracefully in a crouch in front of her white, modern desk. The white interior and clean lines of the room were such a relief from the old, dark, and uneven castle rooms. The quiet and the calm did not last for long as the phone lines began to buzz with urgency. The downside to being the boss, Lexi thought to herself, that any hiccups fell to her to cure. Lexi had to admit that she did love it, being in charge, solving problems, and working hard. Not many people can say they love their jobs, but Lexi loved her job. She was good at it, and she had worked damn hard to get to the top, shattering glass ceilings as she went. Her company had made the FTSE 100 list for the past three years, and the scholarship programme she had stared at the local university had given rise to some impressive talent. Lexi looked around her minimalist office taking a moment to appreciate the awards cabinet with pride, before she made her way to sit confidently at her desk. She sat down, back straight, eyes forward ready for the onslaught of phone calls and messages awaiting her.

"You have reached Lexi Garmund, of Garmund Dynamics, how can I help you today?" Lexi answered the first phone call with perfect professionalism. She had started her company straight after graduation in 1998, with a folder of ideas and plans, and after a few years of struggles and hard graft it had turned into a well-oiled machine. By now she knew everything there was to know about aeronautical engineering, she supplied the German armed forces with aircraft and drones, and she was even branching out into virtual reality technology. The latter seemed to bring with it the occasional Twitter troll, and some unpleasant hate mail, but Lexi refused to let a few idiots hold her back. If anything the venom they spewed simply spurred her on, she was determined to be the best in spite of them, and she was succeeding.

When the clock finally signalled the end of the work day Lexi headed to her private lab. The lab was her space to create, to remind herself why she started the business, to feel the joy and the magic again. Little bubbles of excitement rose in her belly at the anticipation. Lexi had been working on a secret project for the last few months, one that she was finally making headway on. Following in the footsteps of Gabe Garmund, Lexi had been tinkering with the Tairseach technology. She had inherited some of Gabe's plans, passed down through the generations of Garmund's, but no-one had thought them to be that special until Lexi stumbled across them in an old box. She had marvelled at how brilliant Gabe must have been, a twinge of sadness at never having had the chance to meet him, they would have had a lot in common she imagined. Perhaps they would have had more in common than she had had with her parents. Lexi had never felt like her parents understood her, her passion for science, or her creative hobbies. They loved her sure, but they never made an effort to really know her or to be a part of her world. Gabe's plans had filled in some gaps she had been missing about how the Tairseach worked, how it could be harnessed to make it more effective, and had revealed a helpful tip on recreating the portal pocket that protected the castle.

Lexi was fed up of always being a step behind Bas, and she was fed up of being constantly worried about her own safety and that of the Cosantóirí. She may not show her affections outwardly, Lexi thought to herself, but she cared deeply for the Cosantóirí and she wasn't going to stop until she had figured out how to keep them all safe. So every evening after work Lexi came down to the lab determined to make a breakthrough.

"Tonight. Tonight is the night." Lexi announced to the empty room as the fluorescent lights flickered on.

*****

The feather touch of soft sheets embraced Skyler as he landed like a starfish on his bed, the duvet ruffling up around him as he lay there. He didn't want to move, the memory foam mattress knew his shape, and it held him, willing him to drift off to sleep. But the thought that Shura was halfway across the world from him was oddly disconcerting. Though he knew she was safe, and could more than handle herself, Skyler had to admit he missed her presence. As kids they had been constantly at odds, always vying for their Father's attention, and so different in their approach to the world. But when their Dad died,

Skyler could remember how broken they both were and how they had realised they needed each other. Since then they had been almost inseparable, sure they fought like all siblings do, but they always had each other's backs. Being raised by a single Dad had made them both strong and independent, but Skyler felt like he had to take over the role of protector when their Dad had passed.

Skyler always teased, and joked and jested, because he couldn't stand the thought of Shura being as sad as he sometimes felt. But fifteen was a young age to suddenly be expected to be completely self-sufficient, to become a part of a secret legacy, to learn how to survive the real world and the worlds that no-one else knew about. Skyler's phone buzzed loudly, vibrating across the bedside table enthusiastically. He reached out and caught it before it dropped to the floor. He smiled to himself with relief, he certainly couldn't afford to replace it again, that would be his third one this month. Skyler looked at the reminder flashing across his phone screen.

Drink & Bell, 8pm Shift.

"Shit!" Skyler cursed with annoyance. "I'm too tired to work a late shift at the pub." he implored at the ceiling, raising his arms in frustration.

*****

Izzy's bare feet touched the cool surface of the patterned floor tiles, a familiar feeling as the warm Egyptian air wrapped around her skin. Returning home was always an anti-climax for Izzy since her parents had passed it was just her, alone in this large orange house. She would much rather be spending time with the rest of the Cosantóirí, even if they argued a lot, they were her family now. Izzy danced over to her desk, it faced out of the open window, her view to the beautiful colours of the world outside her house. In the distance she could see two worlds divided by a single street, to the left were busy streets filled with cars and bright lights, and to the right she could see the vibrant markets thrumming with people. This is where she sat whilst she wrote, poetry mainly, but she was working on a short story too. She loved to write, as soon as she put pen to paper she entered her own world where anything was possible. Izzy could just disappear into the pages, the time flying by without her even noticing. On the days when she struggled to find anything to say she simply had to look out of her window, there was so much going on it gave her inspiration, it showed her that there were plenty of other people's stories to tell. If that didn't work, Izzy would go for a wander through the market taking in the aromatic spice mountains, and touching the delicate silks hanging in every shade. The world had so much to tell her, she just had to listen to it, and likewise, Izzy had so much to tell the world too.

As she sat at her desk Izzy watched as a group of kids played in the street. They kicked a football between them as they bounded between the houses. It made Izzy slightly envious, she had never had that kind of childhood, she had been in the Cosantóirí since she was thirteen. Watching them play together, joking with each other, picking one another up when they fell over, it made Izzy long for a sibling or at least a friend her own age.

*****

Hector stepped confidently into his modest kitchen, chuckling to himself. He always felt like the parent, or the grandparent, to the rest of the Cosantóirí. He loved that they had become like family, but he also felt the weight of the responsibility of being a parent figure. Hector headed straight for the stove, placing the kettle atop the flames. There was a reason Hector had chosen to not have his own children, he had seen the worst the world had to offer, and he could never bring himself to bring a child into that world. He would have been good at it, he thought, fatherhood, he would have loved the child more than anything. He would have shared his joy of reading, taught them to be proud of their roots, to see the beauty in nature, and he would have encouraged them to do whatever made them happy. As he poured the boiling water over the tea bag Hector smiled to himself, realising that he was lucky enough to be able to do some of those things for each member of the Cosantóirí. Hector took his brewed tea with him to the garage, he smiled a winning smile as he entered the room. This was where he kept his most prized possession, tucked away under its cream cover. Pulling the cover off, Hector placed his hand gently on the vibrant red paint of his 1966 Fiat Abarth 1000 OTR, patting the machine with pride. He had purchased the little crimson number at an auction a few years ago, it had been a bit worse for wear back then, but with some love and care Hector had brought the Abarth back to life. He had happily tinkered with the machine, and travelled miles to retrieve parts for the old boy.

*****

76

Alexandra landed unceremoniously on her backside, sliding in reverse across the Chadwick Manor foyer until her back hit the wall with a soft bump. Her mop of curls had covered her face, thankfully hiding her reddening cheeks. Shura on the other hand had landed casually on her feet, like she had just stepped delicately from a train onto the platform. She was staring at Alexandra with amusement, whilst she adjusted the sling to sit more comfortably around her neck. Shura still looked pale, but she looked more frustrated by the sling.

"Well you managed to avoid the table this time, A.C." Shura chuckled, patting the round table in the centre of the foyer emphasising her point. "Now you just need to learn how to land on your feet. But we can work on that." Shura smiled, offering her uninjured hand.

"Thanks. I think." said Alexandra. She took Shura's offered hand and pulled herself to her feet. They both stood for a moment, hand in hand. Alexandra felt very aware of Shura's breath on her skin, her eyes a marvel of green hues up close. Alexandra could feel the heat rising in her cheeks. She took an unsteady step back, brushing dust from her trousers as she composed herself.

"Chadwick Manor is always so impressive. It's not like other places that feel smaller as you get older. No, this place, it always feels big." Shura marvelled, gazing around the foyer.

"You've been here before?" asked Alexandra with an air of surprise. But before she could get an answer Wyatt came striding into the room, his green flannel shirt instantly recognisable. A look of relief graced his face, as he took in Alexandra in her borrowed clothes and Shura in her sling and oversized shirt.

"Welcome home, Miss Alex. I hear you've had an eventful first day as a member of the Cosantóirí." said Wyatt, his tone neutral. "Miss Adelmo. It is lovely to see you as always." he smiled graciously.

"Wyatt! How's it going? It's been a while." Shura replied. To Alexandra's surprise the two of them fist bumped. Alexandra tried to contain her laughter at Wyatt fist-bumping another human, it was not something she ever expected to witness.

"A.C why is your face doing...that?" Shura asked, pointing at Alexandra's face which was unsuccessfully holding in her emotions. Alexandra's mouth was a thin line, and her eyes were glistening with restrained laughter. Finally her lips gave in resulting in an awkward snorting laughter noise.

"It's just...this. This is funny." Alexandra replied. Waving her hand at the two of them to emphasise her point. Alexandra was aware that she was probably coming across as slightly insane right now, and she could feel Shura and Wyatt judging her, but she headed towards the kitchen still giggling to herself anyway. Maybe the fist-bump had been the final straw to tip her over the edge Alexandra thought to herself.

*****

"A.C it's freezing out here." Shura said stepping onto the icy porch with a thick woollen blanket wrapped around her shoulders. Alexandra was sat on the porch swing, a glass of wine in hand, watching the snow settle on the grounds. She barely acknowledged Shura as she spoke, lost in her thoughts, and slightly tipsy from the wine. Shura sat down heavily on the porch swing, making it rock back and forth, and startling Alexandra at the same time.

"It is beautiful out here though. Even if I can no longer feel my face." Shura continued unfazed by Alexandra's silence.

"Wine?" Alexandra asked. Finally breaking the silence, and offering her glass to Shura.

"Sure. Why not?" Shura replied, taking the glass from Alexandra and having a sip.

"How's the shoulder?" Alexandra inquired with genuine concern.

"Sore, but I've had worse." replied Shura taking another sip of wine.

"Really? Worse than a dagger to the shoulder?" Alexandra asked. Intrigued by what other death defying moments Shura might have encountered.

"Well, no. But it sounded cool, right?" Shura grinned as she spoke. She lifted the glass to her lips, but Alexandra reached out and plucked it from her hand in mock annoyance. "So not funny then?" Shura retorted playfully. Alexandra responded with a sarcastic glare, and an eye roll.

"How can you be so casual about it all? I mean you almost died today." enquired Alexandra.

Shura paused for a moment, pulling the blanket closer around her, breathing in the cool night air. Shura continued to look out at the snow covered gardens as she spoke.

"Well, I've known that the monsters under my bed were real for a long time now, A.C. Skyler and I have been members of the Cosantóirí since we were fifteen, and the one thing I have learnt in the last ten years is that if you don't laugh about the hard stuff, or find a way to decompress then this work will destroy you. It is true that, it's not every day you almost die, but when it does happen I refuse to let anyone have the power to make me feel sad or afraid. Certainly not Bas. For a moment there it was scary, sure. But Bas doesn't get to control my anger or fear when the moment has passed, and if Bas doesn't have that control then I'm winning." Shura looked at Alexandra as she finished speaking.

She looked strong and confident, and Alexandra couldn't help but be impressed by this incredible woman before her.

"How very evolved of you." Alexandra jested. "I don't think I'm at that stage yet." she continued finishing her glass of wine.

"Maybe not. But give yourself a break, A.C. You've been a member of the Cosantóirí for two days, barely, and you're doing just fine." responded Shura.

She reached for the bottle of wine on the table and poured another glass, drinking a mouthful before continuing.

"After all you did save my life in the last twenty-four hours. That's not bad for a first day." Shura continued.

CHAPTER 6

ALEXANDRA STUMBLED INTO HER room closing the door behind her, the wine buzz was setting in. It had been nice to chat to someone about all the crazy, she thought as she kicked off her jeans and replaced them with pyjama shorts, the temperature in the manor not warranting her usual fluffy winter PJ's.

Alexandra lifted her hoodie off over her head, getting tangled in the sleeves momentarily, and swapped it for a plain white t-shirt. She did not want a repeat performance of the embarrassing elephant tee moment. Unsteady on her feet Alexandra placed her phone on the bedside table, putting it on to charge, when she noticed a reflection of something in the window, a shimmering figure behind her. Before she even had time to turn around, or react, the figure landed a strong kick to the back of Alexandra's knee making her buckle to the floor. The stranger grabbed hold of Alexandra's mass of curls slamming her head, hard, into the table. Alexandra could feel a shooting pain spreading from the point of impact. Her eyes were stinging with tears, and her heart was beating fast with fear. She could feel a throbbing sensation in her head, and her vision was threatening to disappear on her.

Alexandra reached her hand out searching frantically for something, anything, to help her. Her hands made contact with something cold, metal, and sharp - tweezers. Alexandra gripped them tight and with as much power as she could muster stabbed them into the strangers thigh with force. A loud, deep cry of pain echoed from the man's lips as he stumbled back surprised.

"You bitch!" the man yelled in anger. His hood falling back to reveal a blue cap atop his head.

Alexandra struggled to her feet reaching for the lacrosse stick in the corner of her room. She had never really enjoyed lacrosse in high school, she was more of a track and field girl, but she had kept the stick because it had been a gift from her Father when she made the team. Now she was grateful for her hoarder like personality trait. Alexandra took hold of the stick, and spinning around she landed a blow to Mr. Blue cap's face. He hit the deck with a grunt, and Alexandra took her opportunity to run for the bedroom door. She reached out for the handle, but a hand around her ankle pulled her backwards, bringing her to her knees as she tried to stretch for the door. Alexandra kicked out furiously trying to free herself from the man's grasp, but he was strong and he dragged her towards him, pinning Alexandra to the floor with his body weight. The smell of stale smoke made Alexandra feel nauseous as she writhed around in panic.

"Bas has a message for you." the man spoke, his hot breath brushing against Alexandra's cheek. She turned away with a grimace, and tried to push him as far from her as possible. "You should have stayed in Baltimore, Alexandra." he continued.

Alexandra's mind was clouded with fear, she could see no way out, and for the first time in a long time she felt completely powerless. Her ears were ringing and she could feel the heat of her own blood trickling down her forehead. Every inch of her body was screaming, but her mouth was unable to form a sound. The noise of the door opening felt distant and imaginary as Alexandra fought with everything she had to escape.

"And you should have stayed wherever the hell you came from." Shura shouted as she rushed into the room.

She sounded pissed off, and Alexandra had never been so happy to hear one of Shura's snarky remarks. Alexandra was struggling to focus on the room. The events and sounds were bombarding her and she was seeing double as she struggled to take in a full breath. She squinted her eyes, trying to see clearly but it just made her feel sick. Alexandra heard a loud smash, followed by shards of something landing around her and all of a sudden she was able to breathe. The weight that had been pinning her to the floor was gone. Alexandra breathed in deep gulps of air, trying to perfuse her lungs and brain. She looked to the side seeing the man barely conscious on the floor beside her, his head was bleeding and the remains of Aunt Alondra's favourite vase were scattered across the carpet. She looked into the man's eerie blue eyes and was surprised to see the same fear in them that she felt. Then with a flash of light he was gone, the smell of stale smoke lingered as the last reminder of his presence.

"Shit." Shura exclaimed, dropping to her knees beside Alexandra. She placed a hand gently on Alexandra's head, brushing her dark curls free from her bloody forehead. "A.C look at me. A.C, can you hear me? You're okay. You're safe." Shura continued in a softer tone.

Alexandra felt frozen to the spot, unable to take in what was happening. She could feel Shura softly placing a hand on her cheek, turning her face away from where the man in the blue cap had been. Alexandra felt calmer as she locked eyes with Shura, though she could see the concern evident in Shura's green eyes. Alexandra could hear Shura speaking to her in a worried tone, but her mouth was still unable to form words to respond. Loud footsteps were moving quickly up the stairs outside Alexandra's room. Shura's head whipped around ready to fight whatever threat came through the door next. She looked like a warrior in a battle Alexandra thought to herself. The light from the moon was shining on her unkempt blonde hair and creating shadows on her face that made her look fierce. The outline of a familiar figure appeared in the doorway, and Alexandra could see the tension dissipate from Shura's shoulders, her stance relaxing.

"Miss Alex!" Wyatt's voice was filled with fatherly concern. A hint of panic laced his words, a tone Alexandra had only heard once before. Last time it had been when she had broken her arm skateboarding down the driveway. She remembered how her bone had pierced through the skin like a scene from a horror movie, she still had the faint lines of a scar now. Wyatt rushed into the room, taking in the scene of broken furniture and bloodied carpet.

"Miss Alex!" Wyatt implored again. The panic in his words snapped Alexandra out of her state of frozen fear, and she tried unsuccessfully to push herself into a seated position. Her body felt stiff and unresponsive, but she needed to no longer be laying on the itchy cream carpet.

"Here, I've got you, A.C." Shura spoke kindly placing a hand on Alexandra's back to steady her. "Wyatt, do you have an infirmary or first aid room in the manor?" she asked.

"An infirmary?" Alexandra laughed incredulously. "Who has an infirmary in their home?" she said in disbelief, though the question seemed to be being disregarded by both Wyatt and Shura.

"Yes, we have a medical room. It is a part of, what used to be, Alondra's bedroom." Wyatt spoke, ignoring Alexandra's out of place and hysterical laughter. Wyatt and Shura hauled Alexandra to her feet, each draping an arm over their shoulders. They half carried, half dragged her to Aunt Alondra's bedroom and into the walk-in wardrobe.

"This is the infirmary?" Shura inquired raising an eyebrow slightly bemused.

"Of course not, Miss Adelmo." Wyatt responded with frustration. He was entering numbers into a keypad cursing under his breath as a small red light flashed in his face. Finally the red light turned to green, a high pitched beep sounded in greeting, and the shelving unit storing Aunt Alondra's shoes began to slide gently to the right. As the secret door finished moving with a subtle *click*, it revealed an entire room Alexandra had not seen before. It looked like a modern clinic with a bed in the far corner. Metal work surfaces and cupboards, filled with supplies, took up space on the walls.

"Take Miss Alex to the bed please, Miss Adelmo." Wyatt instructed as he headed straight for supplies.

"Sure," responded Shura. She hooked Alexandra's arm over her shoulder and carried her to the nearest bed, placing her gently on its edge. Shura made sure to keep a hand reassuringly on Alexandra's arm to stop her from falling face first to the floor. Alexandra could feel Shura staring at her intently like she was worried Alexandra would keel over at any minute.

"I think I'm okay guys. It's just my head that's a little sore." said Alexandra looking around at the infirmary. "I just need a shower, and maybe a cup of tea." she continued, swaying slightly on the edge of the bed. Her world was swimming somewhat before her eyes, her vision coming in waves.

"I am fairly certain you have a concussion, Miss Alex. And that cut is going to need some stitches." Wyatt replied.

He pointed to Alexandra's forehead as he continued to rifle through a draw full of bandages and cotton pads. Alexandra reached up to touch her head, she winced at the pain, hot blood was sticky on her fingertips as she pulled them away from her skin. Her vision narrowed to a pinpoint, the edges of her eyesight fuzzy, then where there had once been waves of light now there was just blackness and nothing.

*****

Alexandra came too with a pulsing headache, and the odd sensation of how she imagined it felt to be hit by a truck. She forced her eyes open with more effort than usual, feeling confused and disorientated. She could hear the thrum of voices outside of the room, and daylight was forcing its way through the gap in the curtains. Alexandra blinked again realising she was not in her own room, she was wrapped like a burrito in the green duvet of the spare bedroom. She wriggled free from the comfort of the warm bed and made her way gingerly to the door. Her head was sore, and the back of her left leg felt bruised. She looked down to inspect the area, a nasty purple bruise had formed, and her legs were dotted with marks and contusions. As Alexandra reached to turn the door handle she noticed fingerprint bruises on both of her wrists too, her mind flashed back to the blue capped stranger holding her down with a vice grip. Fighting back a nauseous feeling Alexandra shook away the memory and opened the door. She was surprised to find the whole Cosantóirí huddled in the hallway. They were all talking animatedly and it took them a beat to notice Alexandra's presence. Alexandra hated to think what she must look like, because when the team turned their attentions on her they all got a strange look on their faces. They all seemed a little horrified and a lot concerned. Alexandra squirmed uncomfortably at being the centre of attention.

"Alexandra! Glad to see you on your feet." Skyler spoke first, breaking the awkward silence that had begun to grow in the corridor.

"How are you feeling?" Izzy chimed in. Alexandra just stood dumbfounded, unsure of what to say, and still trying to piece together what had happened.

"Why don't we all give Alexandra a minute." Hector suggested. Alexandra was grateful for the save. She watched as Skyler, Izzy, Hector, Wyatt, Raimund, Sascha,

Lexi and Malandra sidled reluctantly down the corridor, and descended the stairs. Shura hung back, she was looking intently at Alexandra, like she wanted to say something important. Alexandra was more than certain that it was a rarity for Shura to be stumped for words, but rarities seemed to be common place lately.

"Thank you." Alexandra said first. She struggled over each word, her mouth was dry and her throat sore, but she finally managed to get the words out. Alexandra did not know how to convey how grateful she was to Shura, for saving her, she just hoped that it was clear in the sincerity of those two words. The two women stood for a moment, a second of calm and understanding, their eyes locked conveying the emotions neither knew how to voice.

"You look like death." Shura replied, ruining the moment as only Shura could. "But, you know I am glad you're okay, A.C." she continued.

Shura placed her hand on Alexandra's shoulder and squeezed it affectionately. "I'll wait for you downstairs with the others, whilst you sort this out." Shura said pulling gently at a matted strand of Alexandra's hair. Alexandra had never met someone who could infuriate and infatuate her in the same breath.

CHAPTER 7

ALEXANDRA COULD NOT REMEMBER a time that she had been more grateful for a shower. She let the warm water run over her matted hair and bruised body, feeling her muscles relax and watching as the blood tinged water turned clear. Alexandra wished that she could just stay in the hot shower forever, but the thought of the rest of the Cosantóirí downstairs mocking the time it took for her to shower had her hurrying to wash the encrusted blood from her curls.

She inspected the array of bruises, in various shades of blue and black, and green and yellow, covering her pale skin. The sight made tears stream from her eyes, all the stress and fear rising to the surface. She rested her head against the tiles on the wall letting the tears fall with the running water. To her surprise she felt better after a good cry. It felt like her body needed to get all the bad out to feel good again.

Alexandra tied her wet hair into a messy bun and hastily chucked on an old shirt and a pair of jeans. She took a look at her face in the mirror; inspecting the thin cut on her forehead and the shadowy bruise on her cheek, but was relieved to see that it did not look as traumatic as it felt. Clearly, Wyatt was skilled at stitching up wounds,

89

all the practice of fixing the hemlines of her school uniforms had paid off. As Alexandra descended the stairs into the foyer she could hear the rest of the Cosantóirí arguing, their voices rising with every step she took down the staircase.

"We should never have left Éan and Claw, we would all be a lot safer there!" Malandra said adamantly.

"That is ridiculous. We have lives to lead. We can't all stay cooped up in the castle forever." Lexi retorted angrily.

"Living in the castle would be fun." Izzy mused attempting, unsuccessfully, to defuse the tension.

"Just because you treat your company like it's the most important thing in the world, doesn't mean that it is, Lexi." Malandra snapped back, furiously. Lexi cursed under her breath in German.

"Ladies." Raimund began, but was swiftly cut off as both women rounded on him.

"Bad move, buddy." Shura whispered to Raimund.

"Why don't we all take a deep breath. Fighting with each other is not helping anything." Hector spoke, having to raise his voice to be heard amongst the rowing.

"Exactly Hector." Skyler smiled in agreement. "We should focus on the fact that both Shura and Alexandra are fine." He said with pride.

Skyler raised his chin in an air of triumph thinking he had calmed the situation.

"Fine is not the word I would use, Skyler. Both of the girls have been through a traumatic event, I can almost guarantee they are not *fine*." Malandra said, air quoting the word fine to enunciate her point.

"One of *those girls* is in the room with you. I can't speak for A.C, but I am fine." Shura jumped in coming to the defence of her brother, and herself.

Sascha was watching the verbal tennis going on around the room; she couldn't decide who was winning, if anyone, as her head went from left to right and back following the play.

"Do you have anything to say, Sascha, or are you just going to sit there looking like a deer in headlights?" Shura asked meanly, instantly regretting her harsh tone. She knew Sascha was shy, and she knew how much she hated group gatherings.

"Shura! Don't take your anger out on Sascha, it is not her fault." Izzy stepped up to Shura, her hands on her hips, she almost looked like a superhero in that stance.

"I'm sorry." Shura said in a softer tone to Izzy. Then she turned to Sascha. "I'm sorry for being an arse."

"You were just frustrated. I get it. I am too, I'm just quieter about it." Sascha spoke softly, smiling reassuringly at Shura.

Alexandra hovered in the doorway for a moment unsure of how to approach the room. She felt like the catalyst to this display of harsh rhetoric and in-fighting.

"This is what Bas wants," said Alexandra as she decided to make her entrance onto the verbal tennis court. "This right here, all of us taking cheap shots at one another. Blaming ourselves, and taking out our frustrations. Bas wants us feeling vulnerable, and afraid, and responsible for the bad crap they do. But it's not our fault, sure we got hurt today, but Skyler is right, we are fine, we are alive, and the only one to blame is Bas." she continued surprising herself at her own confidence.

"You almost died tonight, Alexandra. It's okay to process that." Malandra replied, her voice caring and concerned.

"If Bas wanted me dead, they would have been there to do it themselves. This was a power play. To rattle us." replied Alexandra.

"Well clearly it has worked, mon amie." said Raimund insolently.

"No, we cannot let it. You've all had time to shout, and rant and stomp your feet. Now it's time to make a plan." Alexandra responded adamantly.

"Great speech, A.C. But how do you propose we do that?" Shura asked sceptically.

"Juntos. Together." Hector replied without a second thought. "We need to piece together what we know already, and then find a way to fill in the blanks." He was animated as he spoke, clearly ready to get proactive instead of always having to be reactive. "Why don't we start with the man who attacked you, Alexandra? What do you remember, what did he look like?"

Alexandra pictured the room clear in her mind, the memory coming back to her in frames and feelings. She could feel her hands shaking, so she held them together, trying to hide how terrified the memories made her feel.

"I can't really remember much. It's still all hazy." Alexandra said. She could feel everyone's eyes on her as she tried to recall details of the man.

"He was wearing a blue baseball cap. If that helps. I thought it was strange that he was wearing a hooded jacket and a cap." Shura spoke, taking some of the heat off of Alexandra.

"Right, and he had really blue eyes. I remember because he looked terrified. When I looked at him, he was scared too." Alexandra added, flashes of the attack coming back to her.

"Was he big? With a square jaw?" Raimund asked, concerned.

"What kind of a question is that Raimund?" Shura responded with ridicule. Then she looked at Raimunds face, he was serious.

"Was he?" Raimund asked again with urgency. He looked like he was going to hurl all over the rug.

"Yes. He was taller than Skyler for sure, and he had broad shoulders." Alexandra replied. Raimunds face paled, and he ran his fingers through his greasy hair nervously. He knew exactly who the man in the cap was.

"You know who he is don't you?" Shura accused.

Raimund shuffled uncomfortably, avoiding eye contact with everyone in the room, an impressive feet with eight sets of eyes ogling you.

"Don't you?" She asked again, louder. Raimund remained silent, as Shura's temper rose in tandem.

Wanting answers Shura stood up fast, pinning Raimund against the wall by his collar.

"Do not try to shrug this off, Raimund. What do you know?" Her voice was shaking with fury.

The rest of room looked stunned. Skyler had his hand on Shura's arm trying to pull her from Raimund, and Hector was walking slowly towards the three of them. Lexi and Malandra had stood up fast, but had not moved from their spots, everyone seemed to be unsure of how to react.

"Answer her. Raimund?" Hector said calmly.

Raimund had tears trickling down his cheeks, his nonchalant facade gone. His voice was shaking as he replied. "Yes, I know him.".

Skyler released Shura's arm and whirled around to face Raimund. "Are you in on this? Are you working with Bas?" accused Skyler. Raimund shook his head furiously, as tears continued to pour down his face. He looked utterly broken and ashamed.

"No, no. No. I am not a traitor. Please, you have to believe me." Raimund begged.

"Then tell us. How do you know this man Raimund?" Hector implored.

"His name is Street. He was my brothers dealer." Raimund replied crestfallen.

"That's why you looked so agitated at the castle, when I first met you all. He's your dealer too, right?" Alexandra stated, finally understanding Raimunds odd behaviour. Raimund just nodded, unable to look up from the floor. Shura let go of his shirt, and watched as he slid to the carpet sobbing.

"I didn't know. I didn't know. I swear I didn't know."

Raimund repeated over and over again between sobs. Then the room fell silent, everyone seemed to be processing at the same speed, slowly. Alexandra could feel the awkward tension in the air. To everyone's surprise Sascha was the first one to break the silence. She walked over to Raimund, crouched in front of him and lifted his chin to look at her.

"I think you need some help, Raimund. But you need to ask for it." Sascha stated calmly. Raimund nodded causing fresh tears to run down his cheeks.

"I don't want to be like this anymore." Raimund sobbed. Alexandra could see the innocent little boy that he once was as he sat there bearing his soul to the room.

"Will you help me?" Raimund implored.

"How do we know this isn't just a ruse, to make us feel sorry for you. So we forget that you've been practically sleeping with the enemy." Shura demanded venomously.

Alexandra watched as Raimunds face dropped even further, something she thought was not even possible at this point, and she couldn't help but feel sorry for him.

"Shura!" Sascha shot back like a protective mother bear. "That's unfair. He didn't know.".

"So he says." Shura snarked back.

"I don't believe Raimund would intentionally put any of us in danger, Shura." Hector said, coming to Raimund's defence.

"Well clearly none of us really know Raimund that well at all." Lexi chimed in, finally finding her voice. For once she was in agreement with Shura, an occurrence that rarely took place.

"I think we need to get some perspective here. Raimund did not send this blue capped man, Street, to attack Alexandra and Shura. It is just an unfortunate coincidence that Street is Raimunds supplier, or a well calculated ploy by Bas to create a rift between us. Just because he has an addiction doesn't make Raimund a bad person, it is a disease. One that we can help him fight, I might add." said Malandra in an attempt to be the voice of reason.

"What makes you so certain he's not a bad person? Or that we can help him?" Shura asked angrily.

"Because I've known Raimund since he was eight years old. I can still see that terrified little boy sat here." Malandra pointed to the devastated Raimund. "Don't you see him too? I know your heart is not as cold as you would like the world to believe.".

Shura paused, staring at Raimund for a beat. "I see him. But I don't trust who that little boy has become." Shura spoke softly, disappointment clear in her words. "His selfishness. His actions. They almost killed Alexandra tonight. I can't just brush that aside. I'm sorry."

She finished, her voice breaking slightly. Shura's face was full of emotion as she pushed past Alexandra and left the room.

CHAPTER 8

ALEXANDRA COULD NOT BELIEVE it was nearly
Christmas. She had been so wrapped up in the Cosantóirí
and the drama that it came with, she had forgotten all
about her favourite holiday. As she stared out of the
kitchen window at the snow dancing and flitting around, a
mug of white hot chocolate in hand, she realised
Christmas would not be the same this year. It would be
her first one without Aunt Alondra.

The magic that Christmas usually brought with it
didn't seem to be there this year. Sure the snow was
falling, Christmas songs were playing on every radio
station, and the odd card had arrived in the post, but
there would be no-one to carry out Chadwick family
traditions with this year. Aunt Alondra would not be
coming bounding into her room at 5am on Christmas
morning with quirky presents and a child-like excitement.
There would be no annual excursion to buy a new
ornament for the tree, and no nights full of board games.

"Miss Alex, you look very lost in thought. Is
everything okay?" Wyatt asked as he pottered around the
kitchen making tea.

Alexandra turned to look at him, watching as he strained the tea leaves into a dainty cup. "It's almost Christmas." Alexandra replied unhelpfully.

"Why, yes it is. I was thinking of making a nut roast." Wyatt pondered.

"It's going to be strange this year." Alexandra spoke as if she had not heard a word Wyatt was saying. "No Aunt Alondra, no family traditions, no magic." she pouted like a spoilt child.

"Ah, yes. It is definitely going to be different this year. But we can still create some magic." Wyatt smiled as he spoke. "Alondra would want us to.".

"It just feels the same as my first Christmas without my parents." said Alexandra softly.

"I know. You have lost a lot, Miss Alex." Wyatt paused for a beat. "You might consider what you have gained this year too. The rest of the Cosantóirí may not be family in the traditional sense, but they are family." He spoke in a comforting tone as if he were speaking to a nervous puppy. "Maybe this year is a time to create new traditions, or maybe to share your traditions with the others?" Wyatt suggested.

"But Christmas is in three days, Wyatt." Alexandra protested.

"Then you best get planning." Wyatt responded. He was grinning to himself like he had just won a bet. An air of excitement and triumph in his step as he left the kitchen.

"You've already invited them all haven't you?" Alexandra shouted after him.

"Maybe." Wyatt replied with a satisfied chuckle. Alexandra couldn't help but smile, this was the little bit of festive spirit she had needed. Her smile soon vanished with the realisation that she had to prep a party for ten people in just three days.

*****

Alexandra now understood why people planned Christmas months in advance instead of waiting until Christmas eve. After fighting through crowds of angry shoppers, avoiding squealing children, and wrestling the last turkey from an angry soccer mom, she was exhausted. She felt like she had gone into battle with the locals and lost. Alexandra still needed to find a Christmas tree, to buy gifts, to decorate the manor, and do a million other little errands. As she lugged the shopping bags up the porch steps Alexandra wondered what on Earth she had gotten herself into, planning a party with zero experience and barely any time.

She made a mental note to get coal for Wyatt for dumping her in this mess. Alexandra stepped through the front door, dropping the mountains of bags on the foyer floor, and shaking the snowflakes from her hair. She stopped, a stunned expression gracing her face, as she marvelled at the large fir tree in the centre of the foyer. The green marvel was wrapped in golden tinsel, with bright white lights glowing all around it, it was adorned with glittering purple baubles and all of the decorations Alexandra had made as a child. There was the little silver reindeer her Dad had gifted her one Christmas, and the sparkling shooting stars she had bought with her first bit of pocket money. It looked as if every ornament Aunt

Alondra and herself had purchased over the years had also found a home somewhere on the tree.

Alexandra's eyes welled with tears, it was magical and beautiful. Presents were wrapped in gold and red paper under the tree, in various shapes and sizes, with labels that read '*Love Santa*'. Atop the tree sat a large silver star, its edges were slightly worn with age, but the glitter still glistened in the light of the room. As Alexandra slowly spun on the spot she noticed the lights and tinsel were not just reserved for the tree, but they also decorated the ceilings and walls all around her. She felt like she had entered Santa's grotto, with tiny bows and candy canes lining the banister rail on the stairs. The smell of cinnamon and gingerbread filled the air making her heart swell with joy. Alexandra followed the aroma of freshly baked gingerbread cookies into the kitchen. To her surprise Skyler, Lexi, Wyatt, and Izzy were all stood in the kitchen. Each of them appeared to have been assigned a role. Skyler was mixing ingredients in a bowl, and judging from the flour stains on his face and clothes, he was the creator of the delicious looking cookies on the counter. Izzy was adding spices liberally to a large saucepan on the stove, and stirring an unidentifiable dish. Lexi was pouring prosecco into glasses and occasionally stirring the mulled wine as it heated. Wyatt was running back and forth around the kitchen, ticking items off of a list as he went. A clatter in the background, followed by cursing, told Alexandra that Shura and Raimund were attempting to hang decorations on every inch of the manor. Clearly they were in the Christmas spirit if they were working together without killing one another Alexandra thought to herself. Though she could hear Shura's clipped conversation from the kitchen which signified she was making great effort to be civil.

"Ah, the guest of honour has arrived." Malandra announced walking up behind Alexandra, Sascha in tow, she embraced her in a warm hug.

"What is all of this?" Alexandra questioned, taken aback by the thoughtfulness of the gesture.

"This is Christmas, Miss Alex." Wyatt beamed at her.

"It is tradition in Germany to celebrate on Christmas eve." Lexi added, taking a sip of champagne.

"I have never celebrated Christmas before." Izzy said excitedly. "My family celebrate Eid in the summer instead," she continued to Skyler's look of confusion.

"My mother, too." Malandra smiled warmly at the memory. "I was lucky enough to get to celebrate both.".

"Alexandra, you're here." Hector announced meandering into the kitchen, he looked slightly tipsy already. "Let the festivities begin." He announced raising a glass in the air.

The ice cubes clinked against the glass musically as the clear liquid swilled from side to side. Alexandra chuckled and raised a glass of champagne in the air with everyone else.

"It has been gin-o'clock all day for Hector." Skyler whispered so only Alexandra could hear him.

*****

Christmas tunes were belting out all around the Manor, every inch of the place decorated with bright lights and twinkling tinsel, as Alexandra watched Hector and

Malandra dancing in the living room. The twins had turned the space into a dance floor, with a makeshift bar in the corner. Lexi and Skyler were talking excitedly at the bar, Izzy was dancing around the whole room like a little sprite, whilst Raimund and Sascha relaxed next to the fireplace each with a plate full of snacks. Alexandra smiled at the room as she leant against the door frame, it was so nice to see the house filled with so much fun and light. Everyone had made an effort to dress fancy for the evening from Skyler looking dapper in his suit jacket and shirt, to Hector's full suit with a waistcoat and top hat, then Lexi in a beautifully refined pant suit in a subtle burgundy colour. Izzy's outfit was all bright colours, her headscarf adorned with tiny little stars, whilst Sascha had gone for a more subtle black dress. Even Raimund had dressed the part with his blue shirt tucked into a pair of smart trousers. Alexandra had been surprised by Wyatt, who gifted her with a stunning red V-neck dress. The dress was not something she would usually wear, but it was Christmas so she had obliged, and Alexandra had to admit she felt incredible.

"We're out of mulled wine!" Skyler bellowed across the room, clearly merry.

"Don't worry. I'll get some more from the kitchen." Alexandra shouted back, fighting to be heard over the music.

As she meandered through the foyer and into the kitchen Alexandra thought to herself how genuinely happy she felt for the first time since Aunt Alondra had died. Even if just in this moment, surrounded by music, bright lights, and new friends, Alexandra was happy. As Alexandra walked into the kitchen she noticed Shura, leaning against the kitchen side, staring through the window with a pensive look on her face. Alexandra was taken aback by how beautiful she looked just standing there lost in thought. The subtle golden waves in her hair mixed with the more dirty blonde strands as they tumbled down her back long and thick. Shura's sun-kissed skin made Alexandra long for the beach, and her golden dress sparkled like a shooting star. As Shura turned around, Alexandra could feel her cheeks blush as if Shura could see her thoughts written all over her face.

"Well don't you look stunning in that red dress." Shura marvelled, making Alexandra smile coyly.

"Why thank you. You don't look so bad yourself." Alexandra responded flirtatiously. "How come you're hanging around in here on your own, I thought drinking and dancing would be your kind of thing?" Alexandra enquired curiously.

"I don't know whether to be offended at the assumption, or impressed that you would usually be correct." Shura mocked.

"I would say, be impressed." said Alexandra, walking around the breakfast bar to stand in front of Shura.

Her green eyes sparkled as Alexandra brushed a strand of Shura's blonde hair behind her ear, leaving her hand there for a moment as the two women gazed at each other. Time seemed to stop as Alexandra slowly let her hand drop to her side, she felt nervous, more nervous than anyone had ever made her feel.

"So why usually?" Alexandra asked trying to break the tension.

"It sounds silly, but sometimes I can sense when something is going to happen. It feels like something bad is coming." Shura explained.

Alexandra took a step closer.

"And what about now? What do you sense now?" she whispered, like she was telling a secret. Shura gazed at Alexandra, her eyes following the lines of her red dress down to where her hand rested. She took hold of Alexandra's hand, her touch delicate and soft, but deliberate. Shura raised her eyes slowly to meet Alexandra's.

"I sense something good is coming." Shura whispered back. She placed her hand tenderly at the nape of Alexandra's neck, holding her gently as she pulled her closer. Alexandra took a half step forward, she could almost feel Shura's body touching hers. Shura pulled Alexandra in closer again, and Alexandra could feel Shura's lips brush her own. The taste of champagne was sweet on her lips.

"Alex! Where is that mulled wine you promised me?" Skyler's booming voice called down the corridor, breaking through the moment. Alexandra stepped back from Shura hastily, grinning, she placed her hands on the counter to steady herself. Shura lent against the counter, her back to the kitchen door, as she stared out of the window with a smile that matched Alexandra's. Shura's cheeks looked flushed, and she knew her brother would clock her facial expression and read her instantly. Seconds later Skyler stumbled into the kitchen the wine buzz propelling him forward.

"I am dying of thirst waiting for my wine, Alexandra." Skyler joked theatrically.

"I feel like you probably don't need any more wine." Shura muttered, still not looking at him.

"But it is Christmas dear sister." Skyler sang back with a cheeky grin on his face.

Alexandra plucked another bottle from the wine rack and handed it to Skyler, watching as Shura rolled her eyes.

"But it's Christmas." Alexandra repeated with a devilish smirk.

Skyler grabbed the bottle with glee, bowing in thank you as if she were the Queen.

"Why thank you, Alexandra." Skyler commended. "Also why are the two of you hiding in here when the party is in there." he pointed in the direction of the front room with a flourish. "Come, come." Skyler ushered, taking hold of Alexandra's hand and spinning her to the door whilst pushing a protesting Shura to follow.

"You are the worst." Shura grumbled.

"Or am I the best." Skyler retorted placing his arms around Alexandra and Shura's shoulders and leading them to the dance floor, wine bottle in hand.

The music grew louder as they walked into the living room, Skyler dancing off to the bar with his bottle of wine. Alexandra took hold of Shura's hand and led her to the dance floor to join the others, watching as Skyler topped up Wyatt and Lexi's glasses with more wine. Lexi laughed and tapped Wyatt on the shoulder playfully as if he had just told the most hilarious joke in the world, Alexandra almost chuckled at the obvious flirting. Wyatt laughed back shyly, he was clearly enjoying himself which made Alexandra's heart swell. Alexandra scanned around the room at everyone dancing, drinking, and smiling, eventually locking eyes with Shura who was watching her curiously.

"You look happy." Shura smiled.

"I am." Alexandra replied, spinning Shura by the hand as they danced across the floor.

*****

Hector was the first one to turn in for the night, claiming that he had had many more dancing years than all of them, and so he needed more sleep. Skyler was passed out on the couch, the wine having gotten the better of him. Malandra draped a blanket over Skyler then headed to one of the guest rooms to get some sleep. Wyatt escorted a drunk and stumbling Lexi to another spare room, wrapping her in the duvet as she sprawled out face down across the bed. Wyatt placed a bucket at the head of the bed, as Lexi began to snore with deep sleep, before he left for his own room, slightly unsteady on his feet. Izzy had drawn the short straw and had been relegated to the sofa bed in the study where she sat writing by flashlight, her eyes heavy but her mind inspired. Raimund and Sascha were still chatting away by the fire, caught up in a lively discussion, and the last ones standing.

Alexandra had ducked out onto the porch to get some air, the loud music and the roaring fire were a little overwhelming after a while. The heating lamps kept the chill from touching her as she breathed in the crisp snowy air, the stars twinkling brightly in the navy sky. Alexandra turned as the door creaked open, her smile bright against the darkness of nightfall, as Shura stepped out to join her on the porch. She tiptoed across the wooden floor towards Alexandra with bare feet, coming to a stop beside her. Shura's arm brushed Alexandra's making her heart beat faster and her body shiver.

"Are you cold?" Shura asked concerned, moving her hand to cover Alexandra's.

"No." Alexandra replied, her deep brown eyes glinting in the moonlight with anticipation.
Alexandra moved in closer so their lips were almost touching. Then Alexandra could feel Shura's warm lips against her own, the heat coursing through her body like a bolt of lightning. Alexandra moved her hands to hold Shura closer, one hand at her lower back the other laced through her golden hair, as the kiss deepened. She felt dizzy, as if she were drunk, a euphoric feeling engulfing her as Shura's hand slid to her waist, and then to the hem of her dress.
Alexandra's breathing deepened as Shura's hand touched the bare skin at her thigh, pulling her body into hers. Every kiss, every touch, every breath on her skin sent shivers down her spine. Alexandra ran her fingers gently across the bare skin at Shura's collar bone until they reached her dress strap, lacing her fingers under the cotton of the dress Alexandra began to slide the strap delicately down Shura's arm.

Alexandra paused for a moment, waiting for consent to continue, as she looked into Shura's animated olive green eyes.

"Are you sure?" Alexandra asked, her heart beating fast.

"I am." Shura responded, pulling Alexandra's crimson lips against her own in a passionate kiss.

Alexandra freed the straps of Shura's golden dress from her shoulders until it hung at her waist, the delicate white lace of her bra glowing against her tanned skin. Alexandra pushed Shura up against the wall of the Manor, her hands placed on her exposed skin trying to understand every inch of her beautiful body. Alexandra could feel Shura's fingers tugging gently at the edge of her underwear until they were inside her, pleasure coursed through her body, her breathing rapid as she climaxed. Alexandra kissed the other girl hard, working her way down her neck, to her breasts, reaching her hand under her dress as she went. Alexandra slid Shura's silk underwear down her smooth thighs to the floor, casting them aside. She placed a gentle kiss on Shura's inner thigh feeling her skin shiver under her touch. Alexandra sank her teeth into Shura's exposed flesh, causing her to let out a squeal of surprise. Her hands placed on the back of Shura's thighs Alexandra explored her body with her tongue. Shura moaned with delight, one hand braced on the windowsill, her nails digging into the paint, the other hand grasped Alexandra's glossy hair. Shura could feel the other girls tongue working a magical rhythm setting every nerve in her body on edge. Shura was breathing deeply, her hand tangled in Alexandra's raven curls as she pulled her lips back to her own.

Shura's free hand slipped under the V-neck of Alexandra's red dress cupping her breast, she could feel Alexandra's body respond as she fondled her bare skin. Every breath was visible in the night air, as the cold began to fight its way through the heat. Alexandra could feel the warmth of Shura's skin, a distinct contrast from the polar temperatures surrounding them, as their bodies intertwined.

"Wow." Shura exclaimed breathing hard. "What a way to see in Christmas." she joked grinning as she leant against the wall, her hands holding onto Alexandra's waist keeping her close.

"This should definitely be a Christmas tradition." Alexandra teased.

"I vote a warmer climate though, I can't feel my toes." Shura jested, her body now shivering from the cold.

"You're freezing!" Alexandra stated, helping Shura re-dress as her teeth started to chatter from the Baltic temperatures. "I have an idea." she whispered moving towards the front door of the manor, and ushering Shura to follow. Alexandra peered around the edge of the door, the house was quiet and still. "Follow me." she whispered to Shura taking her by the hand and leading her through the manor. They ran through the foyer, trying to be quiet, but struggling to mask their giddy laughter.

"Where are we going?" Shura asked in a hushed tone.

"To a warmer climate." Alexandra replied audaciously.

*****

Alexandra was awoken by a ray of sunshine breaking through the gap in the curtains. The sky looked bright blue and clear from the tiny slither of the outside world Alexandra could see from the bed. She could feel Shura's arm resting across her waist as she lay on her back, a smile played at the edge of her mouth as she remembered the night before. Shura was sound asleep with her head buried in the pillow, her blonde hair a wild mess hiding her face. Alexandra carefully moved Shura's arm, sliding out from under the covers, trying not to wake her. She grabbed some clean clothes from the mound on the chair in the corner, hastily chucking them on, and snuck out of the room. Alexandra quietly closed the door behind her, the smell of fresh food welcoming her into the hallway and following her all the way to the dining room.

"Merry Christmas!" Alexandra announced as she walked into the room.

"Merry Christmas, Miss Alex." replied Wyatt as he dished up an impressive array of breakfast foods.

"Do you have to be so loud?" Lexi moaned rubbing her temples with her fingers.

Skyler mumbled something unintelligible, that sounded like agreement with Lexi, his head resting on his arms against the table. Izzy giggled at their sorry state, clearly amused.

"Champagne, Miss Garmund?" Wyatt enquired playfully, watching as Lexi's face turned an unnatural shade of green. She raised her hand to decline the offer, her eyes conveying her contempt.

"Don't be cruel, Wyatt." Alexandra chuckled.

"I don't know what you mean, Miss Alex. I am simply being a good host." Wyatt grinned devilishly.

"Morning all." Shura announced, stifling a yawn in the process. "Those look fantastic." she continued pointing at the spinach and cheese breakfast muffins.

Shura placed a hand lightly on Alexandra's shoulder as she reached across to grab a muffin. "I feel like I've worked up quite the appetite." Shura said in a lowered voice. Alexandra felt her cheeks flush, as she tried not to grin like an embarrassed teenager.

"Where is Sascha, still asleep?" Alexandra asked the room trying to mask her glowing cheeks.

"I believe she woke early and headed home to feed Demetri." Raimund announced as he sidled into the room.

"Her cat." Hector added in response to Alexandra's confused face.

"Wyatt, the breakfast spread is very impressive." said Raimund clearly excited to get stuck in.

"Thank you, Mr Delmira." replied Wyatt. "I'm glad you approve."

CHAPTER 9

THE SMELL OF CHILLIES and cumin filled the kitchen as Sascha stirred a bubbling pan of tomato based sauce adding an array of vibrant spices as she went. She was singing along to Alabama Shakes as she stirred in a mixture of beans and vegetables. There was something so comforting about the smell of five bean chilli, it was a perfect winter warmer, and her own holiday tradition. She didn't think the others would appreciate chilli on Christmas day, so she decided to enjoy her own batch and then head back for the rest of the festivities. Sascha had forgotten how nice it was to spend the holidays with company, with human company she corrected herself in her mind.

"Demitri! No." Sascha scolded. The cat was nibbling the edges of the freshly baked bread on the kitchen side. He meowed loudly in annoyance as Sascha shooed him off of the side. "It's not food time for you yet Demetri." said Sascha, watching the cat slink into the next room.

Sascha wrinkled her nose at the sudden unexplained smell of perfume in the room. It smelt like lily's and something she couldn't quite place. It was overpowering the smell of spices, making the air smell strange and not the least bit comforting. Sascha reached across the counter to close the window, hoping that the aroma was simply wafting in from outside, when she paused sensing a presence in the room.

"Well doesn't that food smell exquisite. I must admit I am a little peckish after my journey here. The holiday traffic is just dreadful." the woman spoke in a soft voice.

Sascha spun around, dropping the sauce covered wooden spoon on the floor in surprise. The masked intruder was holding Demetri in her arms whilst he protested with a hiss. The silver mask made the woman's features look strong, her cheek bones standing out in the almost pointed metal. Her hair was hidden under a dark hood attached to the mask, the thought of wearing such a thing made Sascha feel claustrophobic.

"How did you get into my home?" Sascha asked in a fierce tone. Her panic levels were slowly rising, and her need to grab Demetri from the strangers arms and run was almost overwhelming. Sascha reached slowly behind her back, hiding her actions from the masked figure, as her hand closed around the handle of the sharp knife on the side. She held it behind her, poised ready for when the moment came to strike. The lady in the mask let out a cruel laugh.

"Oh honey, don't you know who I am?" she asked.

"I have no idea, and I have no desire to know." Sascha replied with more confidence than she felt. "You need to leave, now." she continued, her voice rising with the last word.

The lady laughed again, but this time it was laced with anger.

"Well, Sascha. I know exactly who you are. It seems only fair that you know who I am before I kill you." her voice was shaking, as if she was struggling to control her irritation. She spoke as if Sascha was simply a nuisance in her own home. "Most people call me Bas," the masked woman continued in a calmer, sickly sweet, voice.

Sascha could feel the colour drain from her own face with terror. Demetri must have sensed her fear, because he lashed out digging a large gash into Bas' forearm leaving a trail of blood. Demetri leapt from the woman's arms running straight for the open window in the kitchen. Clearly loyalty and protection were not his priority Sascha thought distantly as she steadied herself, planning a way out if this situation. Or maybe the cat just knew when he was already beat. Sascha reached up reflexively to the key at her throat, only to realise with horror that it was not there. She racked her brain as to where she would have left it, she very rarely took it off.

"Looking for this, my dear?" Bas enquired mockingly, dangling the key from her fingertips. "You really should remember to put it back on after you shower, you silly billy." her sticky sweet southern twang went right through Sascha, making her shudder.

Whilst Bas was distracted by the key, Sascha decided it was time, and with a swift flick of her wrist she hurled the knife fast and sure at Bas. It struck her in the shoulder with perfect accuracy. Bas stumbled back from the force, recoiling in pain and letting out an almost inhuman shriek. Bas seemed to recover quickly, letting out a short cackle, she gritted her teeth and pulled the knife free dropping it to the floor without a second thought.

"Well, that was just rude, Sascha." said Bas. Her breathing was slightly heavier as she tried to disguise her pain. Bas began to walk towards Sascha, her eyes ablaze with anger. Sascha picked up the saucepan from the stove and launched the piping hot contents in Bas' direction. The thick sauce splattered across the kitchen, causing Bas to pause momentarily.

Sascha picked her moment to run for the door, but before she had even made it out of the kitchen Bas was stood in front of her. Sascha was startled by how fast the other woman was, and then by how strong she was. Bas wrapped her bony hands around Sascha's arm and twisted, hard. A sharp pain bolted up Sascha's arm as her wrist broke with a sickeningly loud crack. Sascha dropped to her knees as Bas continued to squeeze her arm cruelly. Tears streamed down Sascha's face at the pain.

"You know, I thought you might put up more of a fight than this, Sascha. I thought that what they all say about you, behind your back, was a lie. That really, deep down you were a tough cookie. But clearly I was wrong. You're pathetic." Bas spat the last words at Sascha like a sharp weapon.

As if the words had injected a shot of adrenaline into her veins and made her stronger, Sascha stood fast and strong pushing Bas against the wall. Bas made contact with the wall, a slight thud echoed around the small apartment as her head connected with the bricks. Bas released Sascha's arm in shock, clutching the back of her head. Sascha cradled her limp wrist, it was pulsing and turning an unnatural purple-blue shade.

"You bitch!" Bas screamed, losing all control.

"You took the words right out of my mouth" Sascha retorted.

She was trying desperately to hatch an escape route, but feeling increasingly like a mouse in a trap. Sascha decided Demetri's exit was probably her best bet, but as she made her way towards the open window she could hear Bas' heavy footsteps running at her with rage. Everything that happened after that occurred in a blur. Sascha heard a high pitched howl, like a creature in agony, only to realise the noise was coming from her own mouth. Her entire body felt numb, except for an intense pain in her lower back, where her skin felt hot as though her flesh had turned to embers on a fire. Sascha dropped to the floor, as if she no longer had control of her own body, she was blinking hard through tears staring at Bas. She could feel warm, thick, blood filling her mouth and dripping to the floor as she struggled to take in air. Bas stood over her, a bloody kitchen knife in her hand, and cold blue eyes filled with satisfaction and hatred.

"To think you practically handed me your own murder weapon." Bas scoffed, tossing the knife to the floor next to Sascha.

"To think, by killing me, you signed your own death warrant." Sascha spoke in a strained voice, blood spraying from her mouth. "The Cosantóirí will come for you." she finished, her breathing laboured.

"I'm counting on it." Bas replied with unnerving confidence. She dangled Sascha's Tairseach key from her fingers, inspecting it with a bored curiosity, before taking it in her fist and burying it in her pocket.

*****

"Miss Alex? I have something for you." Wyatt spoke in a hushed tone not wanting to startle Alexandra. His arms were hiding something behind his back as he watched Alexandra scrub the last plate clean. She had offered to

116

do the tidy up, since it was Christmas and Wyatt always did so much for her. It was a small gesture, but Wyatt adored the love behind it. Alexandra wiped the soap suds from her hands, and turned to look at Wyatt. Her face was a mix of eager anticipation and confusion.

"How intriguing." Alexandra replied excitedly. She pulled up a chair, to the breakfast bar, and sat.

"Don't get too excited. It is only something small." Wyatt said shyly.

He revealed a small box from behind his back, it was adorned with tiny silver reindeer and wrapped in a bright orange bow. Wyatt handed Alexandra the box and ushered her to open it. Alexandra carefully untied the intricate bow, placing it on the table, and easing open the mysterious box. A huge smile spread across Alexandra's face as the mystery of what was in the box was revealed.

"Oh, Wyatt. It's beautiful." Alexandra declared, taken aback. She held the delicate ornament in her palm. The glass object had been moulded into a wintery icicle, and it's translucent exterior made the light bounce off of it. Tiny, barely visible, stars had been etched into the surface too.

"I thought this was one tradition we could keep in the family." Wyatt smiled sincerely, his eyes welling up slightly.

"I think that is a great idea Wyatt." Alexandra replied, embracing Wyatt. "Do you want to help me find a spot on the tree?" She asked with childish excitement.

"I would be honoured, Miss Alex." Wyatt beamed.

Ring. Ring. Ring. Ring.

"What is that?" Alexandra asked as an incessant ringing tone filled the manor.

"That is the landline phone, Miss Alex." Wyatt said, a hint of mockery in his voice.

"People still use those." Alexandra joked.

Wyatt simply rolled his eyes and shook his head, chuckling to himself as he headed to the foyer to answer the phone.

*****

Shura breathed in the icy air as she jogged down the driveway and into the forest of trees. Their icy branches were frozen in a glistening archway as she picked up the pace. Every branch tip was decorated with a glassy water droplet frozen in time. She could feel the early evening cold hitting her skin, and she relaxed her shoulders enough to let the winter air fill her lungs. Shura had always enjoyed running, she loved that to be good at the sport you had to be completely in tune with your body. You had to know when to push and when to hold back, to rely on and trust yourself and your instincts. It required a steady sense of calm to control your breathing, but a willingness to push the rest of your body to the limit to hit your personal best.

Focusing on putting one foot in front of the other helped to clear her mind, and to calm the stresses in her life. Out here she was completely in control. If she worked hard her times would be great, if she slacked off they would not be. Shura no longer had to think about any of this whilst she ran, the calm, the speed, the endurance, it all came naturally to her.

Headphones in, blocking out the noises around her, Shura could run for miles completely focused and contained in her own slice of the world. She needed that calm today, something felt off to her, she couldn't place the source of the feeling, that feeling that something bad was coming. Christmas Eve had distracted her from listening to her gut, it had been fun and she had felt good, but now she could hear her instincts again and they knew a storm was coming. So she was out in the freezing cold, on Christmas Day, hat pulled down over her ears and hoodie zipped up to her chin, running on crunchy leaves and mounds of snow chasing some perspective. She noticed the distinct lack of woodland creatures, or anything else living, as she continued her journey through the forest. Clearly the animals were smarter than her, she thought, they were probably huddled up in the warmth waiting for the ground to thaw. Shura rounded a tight corner, leaving the cover of the trees and running out onto the snow covered fields, she was amazed that all of this land was a part of Chadwick Manor. Momentarily distracted at the thought Shura hit a patch of solid ice that wiped her feet out from under her. She hit the ground with a thud, the snow jumping as she landed, and her feet digging in enough to reveal the dirt underneath the blanket of powder.

"Damn it." Shura cussed to herself. She could feel the snow melting through her leggings, and dripping into her trainers, causing her to shiver. "That is going to leave a bruise." she muttered to the ground. Shura stood up shaking the ice from her clothes and the stiffness from her limbs. "I guess that's a sign to head back to the manor." she sighed, setting off to run again.

Her pace was slower on the climb back to the manor, partly due to the incline and partly due to the fact she wasn't overly keen to return. Shura could still feel it, that dread that sits in your stomach, a gut instinct, intuition, a sixth sense of sorts. The Manor was in sight, and as she drew closer she could see a familiar figure stood on the porch. Flashbacks to their night on the porch brought a smile to her face momentarily. Shura slowed to a walk, taking in deep gulps of air and stretching her arms out. She could see Alexandra's familiar curls, the colour of ravens, waiting on the porch for her, the girls face did not say that she was about to be the bearer of good news. In fact it said the complete opposite.

"Would it be too obvious to run back to the forest at this point?" Shura asked herself, whispering under her breath.

She was not ready for whatever bad news was coming. Alexandra lifted her hand in a sort of half wave greeting giving Shura the answer to her question. There was no turning back now. She jogged up to the porch steps, stopping at the base of the first step to stretch out her legs, gearing up for the bad news storm.

"Good run?" Alexandra asked. Her voice sounded oddly quiet, and uncharacteristically timid. Shura watched as Alexandra sat on the top step, and she got the sense she should probably join her.

"Yeah. It was a little bit icy. May have hit the deck once, but still good." said Shura counting out her last stretch.

"Good. I'm glad." Alexandra replied half-heartedly.

"You should probably sit, or something." Alexandra gestured to the paint peeling porch step beside her.

"Something has happened, hasn't it?" Shura said knowingly. "You should never play poker, A.C. Your face gives your thoughts away." she tried at humour but her heart wasn't in it.

Alexandra looked uncomfortable as if she was fighting a battle inside her head. She took hold of Shura's hand, placing it between her palms. "Sascha was attacked last night." she said finally.

"What? Is she okay?" Shura spoke before Alexandra could get another word in.

"No. Shura, Sascha is in surgery and the doctors aren't sure that she will make it." Alexandra replied as silent tears laced their way down her cheeks.

Shura was frozen to the porch step, the storm had hit and she wasn't ready for it. Her mind struggled to process Alexandra's words, until finally they melted through the fog in her brain. Shura slammed her fist into the floor beside her, her eyes filled with tears.

"Shit!" Shura exclaimed. "I knew something was wrong."

"Shura!" said Alexandra with concern.

She reached across to take hold of Shura's now bruised hand. Inspecting her grazed knuckles with worry.

"I should have listened to my gut, I could have been there." Shura replied desperately.

"And if you had, if you were, you might be exactly where Sascha is now." Alexandra held Shura's hand gently as she spoke. "No one saw this coming, Shura." Alexandra continued softly.

She placed her hands gently on Shura's shoulders, turning the girl to look at her, making sure Shura heard her next words.

"This is not your fault." stated Alexandra. Shura covered her face with her hand as the tears trickled down her cheeks, leaning into Alexandra for comfort. Alexandra wrapped her arms around Shura wishing that her arms could protect her from this pain, but knowing that they could not.

"Miss Alex, Miss Adelmo. Hector has requested that the Cosantóirí convene at the Hospital." Wyatt's words were gentle as he spoke, standing in the doorway of the manor with red eyes and a solemn face.

*****

Alexandra could see the bad news written on Hector's face, and in the slouch of Raimunds shoulders, as she and Shura walked into the hospital waiting room. Shura must of sensed it too, because she stopped in her tracks like she was deciding whether or not to run towards or away from the inevitable. Skyler stood up and strode towards his sister, wrapping his arms around her, his face looked tired and strained, the usual joy missing.

"She didn't make it. I am so sorry, Shura." Skyler spoke softly

Alexandra felt her heart stutter like she had just been shot with an arrow, breathing suddenly felt like a challenge as tears welled in her eyes. She leant against the wall behind her, an image of Sascha and Raimund dancing at Christmas flashed into her thoughts, Sascha had been smiling and laughing and happy. Alexandra could feel anger threatening to burn through her skin, replacing the sadness, what kind of a monster could hurt someone so kind and caring, it didn't seem fair.

"What happened?" Alexandra asked with despair.

No one seemed to be in a rush to answer her question. Lexi stared at the floor, unmoving, like a grief stricken statue. Malandra covered her mouth with her hand, as if she was holding her words in, tears falling silently to the floor. Raimund placed a comforting hand on Izzy's shoulder as she rocked slowly back and forth. Alexandra looked around the room at them all, they looked broken, defeated, and another arrow of sorrow buried itself in her heart.

"Bas happened." Hector replied, his voice shaking with anger. "It is by the grace of God that Bas was unable to find Sascha's Tairseach. Though my heart wishes her grace had extended further." He paused for a moment, as if he were sending a prayer and asking for this all to be a terrible dream. "I think it would be safest if we all moved into Éan and Claw." he continued. It wasn't a question, but Lexi began to protest.

"We talked about this before Hector..." Lexi began, her voice strained.

"I refuse to lose any more of my family." said Hector cutting Lexi off mid-sentence. His words were final, the decision made.

"What about the Tairseach?" Izzy asked tentatively. "They will be vulnerable without us." she continued with concern.

"I may have an idea about that, and also a small confession to make." Lexi interjected. Everyone turned to look at her, their faces not quite sure what to expect. "I have been going over some of Gabe Garmund's notes, the ones he kept in the family. I think I have pieced together how he created the portal pockets, and how he originally transported the Tairseach." she continued proudly.

"I thought that knowledge had been lost many years ago." Hector pondered.

"Well it was, but I found his work a few months ago. And I've been working on the portal technology since then. I am fairly certain I will be able to transport each of our Tairseach into the castle." Lexi smiled triumphantly. Though the smile faded quickly, and she returned to stone once again with the realisation that one Tairseach no longer had a protector.

CHAPTER 10

IT WAS STRANGE PACKING to move into a castle. Alexandra felt like she was about to be locked in the highest tower, of the tallest castle, without the option of a heroic rescue. She knew it was ridiculous, to feel like moving into a castle was a bad thing, this was what little boys and girls dreams were made of. Plus the rest of the Cosantóirí would be there too, but it just felt so obscure.

Alexandra had already made one giant move - from Baltimore to Rhode Island, and now she was going to Scotland. It was a lot to take in, a lot to process. It had been so difficult to leave her life in Baltimore, to leave Micah behind, to leave her work behind, to leave the life she had created for herself. Alexandra could still picture Micah's face when she told him she wouldn't be back for a while, could hear the disappointment in her bosses tone when she told her she wouldn't be returning to work, and she could feel the cold of her once cosy flat in Baltimore, now empty after moving nearly all of her possessions back to Chadwick Manor. Alexandra had only planned on staying in Rhode Island until after Aunt Alondra's funeral; but then she had seen how sad Wyatt was, and she felt how sad she was, so she had decided to stay - at least for

125

now. Alexandra thought that she might heal better in Chadwick Manor. If she was being honest, leaving her job behind had been a plan for a few months. The work was slow and tedious, and Alexandra felt like her brain was wasting away every day that she spent in that office. It had been an incredible opportunity, and a healthy pay check after college, but Alexandra wanted more. Though she hadn't quite bargained for the 'more' she was currently experiencing.

Alexandra just wanted her world to stand still for a moment, to be able to call somewhere home without the grim reaper appearing and setting her world spinning at warp speed. But, here she was, packing up her life again and moving onto the next chapter. At least this time there wasn't much to leave behind, not like Baltimore. She felt bad for cutting ties with everyone and everything but she hated the thought of anyone getting caught up in what Bas had planned.

The Chadwick Tairseach would be the last to be relocated as Lexi made her rounds moving each portal, to Éan and Claw castle, starting with Sascha's Tairseach. Alexandra was not really clear on how exactly Lexi was going to move the Tairseach, the explanation had flown over her head even on Lexi's tenth try. Lexi had created a device that would absorb the Tairseach power as you stepped through it, taking the Tairseach with you as you travelled to your destination.

"Like taking a teleportation device through a teleportation device?" Alexandra had asked, to Lexi's scorn.

*****

Lexi was always calm under pressure, it was one of the skills that had helped her rise to the top, but today she felt the pressure more than ever before. Maybe it was the weight of her ancestors legacy, the weight of the Cosantóirí who were counting on her, or even the weight of her own need to be the best, Lexi did not know. What she did know was that all of her calculations had to be perfect for today to go to plan. Relocating each Tairseach required exact calculations of the amount of energy coursing through each portal. The separate Tairseach each ran on slightly differing energy levels, so each relocation needed a recalibration of the *'portal porter'* as Lexi had dubbed her new device.

As she stood staring at the Eames Tairseach. Lexi felt nervous. What if the calculations were off, what if she got transported to the middle of nowhere, what if she got stuck in the Tairseach. Lexi paused the 'what if' train of thoughts, they were not useful to her in this moment. Lexi knew the calculations were correct, she had calculated them herself, she was ready. The device was small and sleek, it sat around her palm in a D shape, all smooth curves and matte white material. All she had to do was create a fist when she was inside the Tairseach, this would activate the button on the palm side of the device turning it on, and the portal porter would do the rest of the magic. The device would take in the Tairseach power, collecting it in the device, as Lexi travelled through to the castle. When she arrived at the castle Lexi could then release the Tairseach power reforming the Tairseach in its new location. Lexi looked up to the ceiling before stepping through the Tairseach. *'Wish me luck Sascha.*' Lexi whispered, her eyes welling up slightly. She shook off her emotions and placed one brogue over the threshold and then the other, the familiar array of colours and sounds greeted her, Lexi squeezed the portal porter as she thought about Éan and Claw castle. The Tairseach seemed to push her through to the castle faster than usual, she could feel the power chasing her to the destination, nipping at her heels impatiently. A snap of static whipped through the air as Lexi came to a skidding halt in the basement of the castle, the portal porter was thrumming with energy.

"Did it work?" Izzy asked with excitement as she greeted Lexi.

The group had nominated Izzy to ensure Lexi arrived in one piece. It had been clear at the hospital that Izzy did not want to return home on her own, so this had been Hector's subtle compromise.

"I believe so." Lexi replied with matching enthusiasm.

"Stand back." she instructed. Lexi held the portal porter out in front of her, pointing it towards the far wall, she released her hand feeling the energy fly from the device. The room was aglow with vibrant white light as the Tairseach formed from the bottom up in the basement of the castle. Izzy watched in awe as the light faded and the Eames Tairseach stood in the corner of the room as if it had always been there. Lexi could feel the energy being pulled from her own body as she sat heavily on the floor, removing the device from her palm whilst she regrouped.

"Wow." Izzy marvelled. "That was so cool Lexi!" she exclaimed.

"Yes. I suppose it was." Lexi smiled. "Though it is going to be a long day if one portal transfer takes this much effort." she groaned.

*****

Alexandra had packed, and repacked several times by the time Lexi arrived at Chadwick Manor. Lexi had arrived in the Chadwick basement, where the Tairseach was held. She was unusually unkempt, her hair was frizzy, and she looked exhausted. Alexandra had never seen Lexi look so vulnerable, on most days she was the walking embodiment of confidence and poise.

"Just one more to go." Lexi muttered like a mantra.

"You look exhausted, Lexi. We can wait to transport the Chadwick Tairseach, maybe get some food?" Alexandra suggested.

"No. I am fine. We can eat when we are all at Éan and Claw." Lexi replied stubbornly. "Are you ready to portal?" she asked.

"Yes. All packed and ready to go." Alexandra replied. "How does this work? Do I go first? Do we go together?" she enquired with confusion.

"You go first, then I will be right behind you." Lexi assured her. She gestured for Alexandra to step through the Tairseach. Alexandra tightened the straps on her backpack, and picked up her suitcase. She looked like she was about to travel the world, not like she was about to move into a castle in the middle of nowhere.

"See you on the other side." Alexandra smiled kindly. She stepped into the smorgasbord of lights and sounds, and then she was in the castle basement.

Alexandra was surprised to be surrounded by the rest of the Cosantóirí and their Tairseach. It was eerie how all of the doors formed a circle on the outer edges of the room.

"That was quicker than usual." said Alexandra sounding slightly harassed.

"That's what she said." Skyler chimed in with a cheeky grin plastered on his face. A wave of eye rolls and disdainful looks spread around the room.

"If that's what she said, then you're clearly doing it wrong." Raimund jested back at Skyler.

Before anyone else could get involved, Lexi landed in the basement. She was doubled over on her knees, her face pale and tired.

"Stand back." Lexi instructed, her voice hoarse.

Alexandra watched with surprise as the Chadwick Tairseach was painted out of white light and magic, and materialised in the last remaining spot. She was impressed by how unique each Tairseach looked, they were so intricate and personal, but together they were a wonder to behold. The delicate golden feathers that adorned the Chadwick Tairseach looked so dainty next to the imposing silver sword encrusted with an emerald on the Adelmo Tairseach. The Delmira Tairseach consisted of an incredible opal encased in a triangle shape, whilst the Garmund Tairseach was adorned with subtle purple stars. The Fremont Tairseach housed the head of a spear strong and sure in its carving, so different from the four rubies set in a diamond shape on the Williams Tairseach. The white five petalled mariposa flower of the Sarkis Tairseach told tales of peace and freedom, whilst the thorns wrapping themselves around the Eames Tairseach spoke of protection and power. Alexandra was in awe at their collective beauty.

Malandra helped a reluctant Lexi to her feet, and escorted her from the room. "Let's get you some warm food shall we sweetie." Malandra cooed.

Lexi was clearly too tired to argue, as she allowed herself to be led from the room. The rest of the Cosantóirí followed after them. Hector had organised a giant feast for them all as a 'welcome home' treat, the spread was impressive, and there was enough wine for an entire country. Alexandra had to admit it was nice to be a part of a family meal again, it had been a long time since she had experienced one. But sadness hung in the air like a rain cloud as the empty chair stood out at the table. There was a Sascha shaped hole in the Cosantóirí, and everyone was hurting. Since Sascha had no known living relatives her position would remain vacant, a constant reminder of the deposit they put down to be a part of the Cosantóirí - their lives.

CHAPTER 11

As Hector flicked on the television he scrolled through to find the news. Hector had always been interested in learning as much as he could about the world. The main headline, flashing across the screen, read; '*6 Police Dead After Smugglers Take Their Revenge*'. He rolled his eyes at the insanity of the world.

6 New York City Police Officers were murdered today after drug smugglers staged a break-in to retrieve their confiscated drug supply. The 30 kilograms of cocaine were seized by officers in a successful drug raid just two months prior to the attack. It is unclear if the officers killed were those involved in the original raid. A surviving officer has given a description of one of the suspects, described as a large white male in his 30's wearing a blue cap. The public are being urged to steer clear of the scene, and to report any information to the hotline at the bottom of the screen. The suspects are thought to be armed and very dangerous, police ask that you do not attempt to approach the suspect if seen. Announced the shrill newsreader.

Hector dropped the remote on the table, and ran from the room. He knocked on every Cosantóirí members bedroom door, urging them to meet him in the main hall. Hector thought how crazed he must have looked - out of breath and sweating as he ran between rooms - because nobody argued or protested with him about the fact that it was five in the morning, they simply grabbed shoes and jackets and followed him. Alexandra did not remember there being a television in the main hall of the castle, clearly it was a requisite of one of the members agreeing to move in. She looked around the room at everyone's sleepy faces, the yawns being passed back and forth, and then to Hector. He looked wide eyed and alert.

"There is something you all need to see." Hector announced, turning the sound up on the television.

The group watched as the reporter explained the limited details of the events at the police station, their faces a mixture of horror and confusion.

"This is clearly very sad and all, but why did it require you to wake us all up at five in the morning?" Shura asked, her eyes heavy with sleep and her hair a matted golden mess.

"It's Bas. Isn't it?" Malandra asked, her mind connecting the dots ahead of the rest of the room.

"Yes, I believe so." Hector replied. "Lexi. Alexandra. I need the two of you to travel to the crime scene. I need someone to confirm our suspicions, and to get a look at the video surveillance too." he continued.

"Why me? I don't really have a lot of field experience" Alexandra asked with confusion, putting air quotes around 'field experience'.

"You're American, so you won't draw as much attention. Plus if Street was involved you will recognise him. Lexi do you still have the means to secure police badges?" Hector asked. Everyone looked to Lexi, waiting for a response, both impressed and terrified by her ranging skill set.

"Yes. I can have them ready in an hour." Lexi replied confidently. She still looked pristine, and put together, at five in the morning. Unlike the rest of them who were bedraggled and barely functioning due to sleep deprivation.

"I guess I will put the coffee on." said Raimund, resigned to the fact that no one was returning to the comfort of their beds.

"I definitely want in on the coffee." Shura grumbled.

"Me too." Malandra agreed.

"Me three." Skyler mumbled through a yawn.

*****

"Catch." Lexi shouted to Alexandra, throwing something shiny in her direction.

Alexandra caught the item awkwardly, just saving it from landing in her cereal. She turned the credentials over in her hand, impressed by how real they looked. Alexandra was excited that her face was on an FBI badge, it was not something she thought she would ever see.

"This is cool." Alexandra grinned in amazement.

"I am glad you think so." Lexi responded, pleased with the authenticity of her work. "I will be posing as a German Polizei investigating a similar string of crimes in Hamburg. Alexandra you will be my American liaison. Hopefully we can convince them to let us look at the surveillance tapes".

"I feel like I'm on NCIS, or Criminal Minds, or something." Alexandra said excitedly.

"Such a nerd." Shura teased, bumping Alexandra playfully with her elbow. To which Alexandra simply stuck her tongue out, nothing was going to sour this moment for her.

"Also does this blazer say badass FBI agent, or is it too much?" Alexandra asked smoothing down the collar and buttoning the jacket.

"What you're wearing is fine." Lexi responded in her usual clipped tone.

"Here are the coordinates of a safe place to portal to, outside the station in New York." Hector said, handing Lexi a piece of paper with numbers scribbled on it.

"What will the rest of us be doing?" Skyler asked eagerly.

"I've got some self-defence training plans for each of you. So we will be going to the gym and practising. I want you all to be able to protect yourselves." Hector replied.

"You realise Skyler and I have been black belts since we were fifteen right?" Shura enquired with a grouchy disposition.

"Sí. Just like I am aware that Raimund is a boxer, Izzy is trained in Krav Maga, and Malandra does judo." Hector responded kindly. "The training plans are tailored to your skill sets.".

"Sweet." Skyler said excitedly.

"Are you both ready?" Hector asked Lexi and Alexandra.

"Of course." Lexi replied firmly. Alexandra simply nodded, not feeling quite as confident as Lexi clearly was. Shura and Hector escorted Lexi and Alexandra down to the basement to their prospective Tairseach. Alexandra could see Shura biting her lip nervously.

"You remember the coordinates, yes?" Shura asked. "I don't want you to end up in the back end of nowhere." she shuffled her feet uncomfortably as she spoke.

"You know it's not helping that you look more worried than I feel." Alexandra said nervously. She placed a reassuring hand on Shura's shoulder. "But yes, I do remember the coordinates." she smiled lovingly. To Alexandra's surprise Shura planted a delicate kiss on her lips. Alexandra returned the kiss, excitement pulsing through her veins.

"Stay safe, A.C." Shura whispered so only Alexandra could hear her.

"Are you ready?" Lexi shouted across the room. "This is a time sensitive mission after all.".

Shura rolled her eyes as she opened the Tairseach ready for Alexandra.

"We are ready." she called back to Lexi with a hint of petulance.

"Good luck, and we will see you shortly." Hector stated simply.

Alexandra locked eyes with Lexi, who returned her gaze with a reassuring nod as the two of them stepped through their Tairseach simultaneously. A cold wind breezed through her hair as Alexandra was engulfed by a mosaic of colours and a soundtrack of voices.

Alexandra saw the floor coming this time and managed to land feet first in a rank smelling alley way. She took in a steady breath as a flutter of panic passed through her mind. Was she in the right place she thought to herself? A pulsing in the air nearby confirmed Alexandra was where she was supposed to be, as Lexi landed softly beside her. The familiar American twang echoed from the streets around them and Alexandra realised for a brief second how much she had missed the familiar. Everything around her was constantly changing, but her mind seemed to be one step behind in processing it all.

"We should be just around the corner from the station, according to Hector." Lexi interrupted Alexandra's train of thought. She was looking from side to side, confusion clouding her heart shaped face, her brow furrowed with concentration. "This way, I'm sure." Lexi continued, not reassuring in her convictions.

A few wrong turns, and a couple of strangers directions later, and the 'NYPD' sign flickered above the doorway of an underwhelming building. The crime scene tape confirmed their arrival at the right location. Alexandra's palms were sweating from nerves, they had not really discussed how this was going to go, and she had no clue how to convince well trained officers to let her look at their surveillance tapes. Before Alexandra could ask the burning question, Lexi was striding into the police station as if she had done this a thousand times before. Alexandra followed, attempting to mimic Lexi's confident strut. She caught up to Lexi just as a burly, dark haired man stopped them, his hand outstretched and his face set in a stoic expression.

"Ma'am, this is a crime scene." the officer spoke in a deep monotone.

"DI Lexi Garmund, of the Polizei Hamburg. And this is my American liaison Special Agent Alexandra Chadwick, of the FBI." Lexi flashed her badge in the officers face, she looked calm and composed as she weaved her lie. "I have been investigating a string of similar crimes in Hamburg, Germany. I am here to help however I can, and would be most grateful if you could show me the surveillance footage so I can confirm if this is the work of the crew I am chasing." she looked like she was enjoying this, her posture relaxed and unfazed. Alexandra was not sure if she should be scared or in awe. She felt like a spare part in this scenario, she didn't even get to flash her badge like Lexi, Alexandra simply set her face into a serious look and nodded at the appropriate times.

"My apologies Ma'am, but I need to approve this with my detectives first." the officer replied, his tone full of uncertainty. His face still serious, the officer waved his colleague over. Alexandra could feel her heart pounding in her chest, and she was certain they were going to be made.

"Detective?" Lexi jumped in before either man could speak. "DI Garmund from Hamburg. We would like to see the surveillance to assist in a string of similar cases in Hamburg, Germany." She flashed her badge again, exchanging a sideways glance at Alexandra to do the same.

"Welcome to New York, Detective Inspector, Special Agent." The detective nodded in recognition to them both. "The more information you can give us the better, we are at a loss here. If the tapes are gonna help, have at 'em." the detective continued. He looked awestruck and confused by Lexi, a feeling that Alexandra shared. "Why don't you take them to view the tapes officer." the detective instructed. The officer escorted them to the surveillance room, and set up the tapes for the exact date and time of the attack. "If you don't mind I will leave you to it. I have to attend a talk with my fellow officers about last night's events." he looked solemn as he left the room, the weight of the world heavy on his peaked cap. Alexandra sympathised, she knew the weight of loss and the toll it would take on him.

Lexi sat down in front of the computer screens.

"Are you ready?" she asked. Alexandra nodded, although she wasn't quite sure that she was actually ready. Watching violence on a television show, that you know is fake, is very different from witnessing it in a real life situation. Lexi hit the play button, and they both watched in horror as a group of men and women wearing steel face masks appeared out of thin air. The police officers barely had time to react, as the group led by the blue capped man, Street, fired upon them. The station looked like a scene from a horror movie, with blood and bodies scattered across the floor. Another person stepped into the room from a segment of rippling portal air, her silver mask making her features look sharp and alien. She stepped, unperturbed, over the body of one of the slain officers.

"*Street, go to the evidence locker and grab what we came for. Kill anyone who gets in your way.*" the woman's voice echoed in the hollow room. Street simply nodded like he had been told to go buy bread at the store.

Alexandra felt the colour drain from her skin, as a wave of nausea hit her like an anvil, she had heard that woman's southern twang before. She took an unsteady step back from the desk, leaning heavily against the filling cabinet behind her.

"Are you okay?" Lexi asked with genuine concern.

"I... I know that voice." Alexandra stuttered as she drew in deep breaths in an effort not to vomit across the room. Her mind flashed back to the morning her life changed forever, to the sweet faced blonde who had comforted her, Alexandra grabbed the bin in the corner and hurled her entire stomach contents into it. Lexi placed a hand on Alexandra's shoulder to steady her, pulling her raven curls back from her face, as Alexandra threw up what felt like everything she had ever eaten. Alexandra tried to slow her breathing as every part of her body was screaming with anger, with fear, and with a strange sense of shame. She felt violated.

"I know who Bas is." said Alexandra finally. Tears streamed down her face as Lexi watched with shock.

CHAPTER 12

ALEXANDRA SHUFFLED ON THE spot, nervously tucking her hair behind her ear, as Lexi looked equally as uncomfortable. They had portalled back to Éan and Claw after Alexandra's revelation, a copy of the tapes in hand, and an awkward silence hanging in the air.

"Why do the two of you look like you've just done something terrible and you're not sure how to tell us?" Shura mocked, intrigue in her tone.

"Is this one of those 'what happens in New York stays in New York' kind of moments?" Skyler jumped in, air quoting theatrically, with a cheeky grin plastered on his face.

"The two of you should go into comedy, you would make a great comedic duo, you're hilarious." Raimund said dryly to Shura and Skyler. Clearly impatience was getting the better of him as he rolled his eyes with frustration. Lexi stared at Alexandra trying to urge her to talk with a look.

Alexandra cleared her throat, avoiding eye contact with everyone in the room (a challenging feat she realised).

"So we watched the tapes, and they were as horrific as you all can probably imagine. We identified Street as one of the attackers." she paused with unease.

"And…?" Lexi prompted.

"And. I am fairly certain that I know who Bas is." Alexandra stumbled quickly over the words, hoping that no-one would process what she was saying. She realised she had not spoken fast enough, because the room erupted with questions and noise.

"How do you know?" Malandra queried suspiciously.

"Who is Bas?" Shura and Skyler asked at the same time, solidifying their double act potential.

"Bas was there during the attack?" Raimund sounded concerned.

"How certain is fairly certain?" Izzy asked with confusion.

"Yes. Bas was there at the attack site, but after the actual slaughter." Lexi answered, trying to spare Alexandra from some of the heat.

Hector was remarkably calm, whilst the rest of the room seemed to be imploding. "Alexandra, why don't you explain how you know Bas? I think it would be a helpful starting point." he advised.

"First off, I would like to start by saying that I met this person before I even knew about all of this. I had absolutely no idea who this woman was." Alexandra started, pausing to consider how much detail the Cosantóirí needed to hear. "So, I met her at a party. I recognised her from my local coffee shop back in Baltimore, and we had a few drinks and well…one thing led to another." Alexandra tried to read Shura's expression, but her face was stoic, giving nothing away.

"Her name is Casey Ray, or at least that is what she told me." Alexandra felt nauseous again at the thought of that night.

The memories were hazy at best, which was disconcerting in itself, and she was struggling to fill in the blanks. Alexandra tried not to dwell on the missing memories, afraid of what they might contain, or simply trying to stay sane, she wasn't sure. Alexandra could feel the sting of tears threatening to escape the confines of her eyelids as she struggled to hold them back, she could feel the judgement emanating from the room.

"Let me get this straight. You think that Bas is the same person you had a one night stand with?" Raimund laughed incredulously. "How can you be so certain?".

"I recognised her voice on the video. And don't look at me like that." Alexandra retorted. "If it was Skyler saying he'd had a one night stand you'd be high fiving him, so don't stand there and look at me like I've done something wrong. Because I haven't." she continued with frustration.

Alexandra knew she wasn't really angry at Raimund, but she needed to take it out on someone. She was angry at Casey Ray for duping her, but she was more furious at herself for not seeing it, for letting it happen, for drinking those extra shots.

"You haven't done anything wrong, Alexandra. You couldn't have known who she was, we didn't even know who she was, or that she was even a she." Malandra reassured Alexandra. She turned to Raimund with a stern look on her face. "And you. You better wipe that toxic masculinity off of your face and enter the twenty first century. Sexual autonomy is not reserved for any one gender." Malandra's voice was steady, but with an edge of rage, as she spoke.

Raimund held his hands up in surrender as it dawned on him now was not the time for humour.

"This is a fantastic lead Alexandra. We have been waiting to get a step ahead of Bas, and you may have just put us there." Hector said positively, his resolve to cripple Bas' operations reignited.

"It doesn't feel very fantastic." said Alexandra as she pushed her way out of the room.

She wasn't sure where exactly she was storming to, but she kept walking, up flights and flights of stairs, until she ended up on the castle roof. Her head was spinning, and she had no idea what to do with all of her feelings. She just wanted to scream, to let all of the rage and frustration out. Alexandra pushed the old wooden door, atop the final flight of stairs, open.

Wow. Alexandra exhaled as she took in the panoramic views, and breathed in the cool, calming air.

She walked over to the edge of the roof, and rested her arms on the high wall dropping her head to meet them. Tears had escaped their confines and were slowly rolling down her face, falling like raindrops onto the castle walls.

"Jeez A.C, you are fast when you're pissed off." Shura stated, trying to catch her breath from the many flights of stairs. "You're not about to do something stupid, are you?" she asked half joking, but half concerned. Alexandra jumped with surprise lifting her head from her arms.

"What? No. I just needed some air." Alexandra replied, horrified.

"The front door would have been closer." Shura muttered, feigning annoyance. "Are you alright?" she asked softly, walking to join Alexandra at the edge of the roof.

"I'm so sorry." Alexandra said, heartbroken.

"You don't have anything to be sorry for, A.C." Shura reassured her, placing a hand gently on Alexandra's back. "That sleaze Bas, or Casey or whatever she is called, on the other hand has a lot of explaining to do." she continued through gritted teeth. "I am so sorry she did this to you." Shura continued, her tone filled with emotion. She pulled Alexandra closer resting her head against her shoulder. They stood there for a while in silence, breathing in the calm.

"I don't remember what happened that night. The night I met her." Alexandra spoke quietly, as if the quieter she spoke the less true what she said would be. "It's all hazy and confused whenever I try." she continued, fresh tears rolling down her cheeks as she spoke. "All I know is I met some girl in a bar, had a lot to drink, and woke up in my bed - not alone. And I don't know what to do with that.".

"I know. But you need to know whatever happened that night, you did nothing wrong. It's not on you. It's on her." said Shura. She lifted Alexandra's chin gently until she was looking into her deep brown eyes, and wiped the tears from her cheek. "Do you hear me, A.C.? It's not your fault." Shura spoke with determination.

A flash of light reflected across the water stirring Alexandra from the momentary calm, she looked out at the lake and hills surrounding her, and noticed something approaching from across the grounds. The glint of metal faces sent a shock of horror down Alexandra's spine.

"Bas is here!" Alexandra said, her tone urgent. Shura turned, with confusion, to look at the place Alexandra was pointing. A group of masked figures were making their way towards the castle.

"Shit." Shura exclaimed. "Come on. We need to warn the others." she grabbed hold of Alexandra's arm and half dragged her to the door. Alexandra froze, like a mannequin in a shop front, she couldn't move or speak.

"A.C. Come on! I need you to snap out of it. You can freak out later, but right now I need you." Shura implored desperately. The words thawed Alexandra's frozen limbs, bringing her mind back to the real world, and she took off running down the stairs.

"Why does this castle have to have so many stairs?" Alexandra yelled at the walls as they continued down the seemingly infinite stairs.

"I just want to know, what is with the friggin' creepy masks? Clearly Bas has some issues she needs to work through." Shura shouted between breaths as she followed Alexandra, happy that her training was paying off.

"That is a serious understatement." Alexandra hollered back.

Alexandra and Shura burst through the double doors of the main room, greeted by a room full of startled faces and interrupted conversations. Alexandra doubled over, hands on her knees as she caught her breath, whilst Shura jogged on the spot casually like they hadn't just sprinted the entire length of the castle.

"What on Earth…?" Hector began.

"She is here! Bas. Bas is here!" Alexandra managed between breaths.

"Bas is on the castle grounds, and she brought company." Shura tried to clarify.

The room erupted into noise once again, but this time the air was fraught with panic and fear. Raimund ran his hand through his hair, tugging at it as he did when he was stressed. Lexi seemed outwardly calm, as per usual, whilst Malandra and Izzy were contemplating their internal fight or flight scenarios. Skyler was staring intently at his sister, as if he could glean more information via eye contact.

"Enough!" Hector bellowed to the room. "Panic later. What we need now is a plan.".

"Hector is right. This is what we were born for, what we have trained for." Lexi said proudly.

"I don't remember training for this." Alexandra muttered under her breath. Shura gave her a side glance that translated as *now is not the time for sarcasm*. Alexandra decided to heed Shura's unspoken advice, recalling all she could remember of her kickboxing classes in high school, in preparation for what was coming.

"Raimund. Izzy. I need the two of you to set-up in the basement. You will be the last line of defence for the Tairseach. If you hear Bas, or any of her army coming, I need you to transport the original portal out of here, to somewhere safe." Hector stood in a firm stance as he spoke, commanding respect, but also imploring the two of them to protect the original Tairseach with everything they have.

"Why only the original Tairseach?" Alexandra enquired with confusion.

"Because if the original Tairseach is destroyed, the others will be destroyed too. Their power is linked to the original." Lexi explained, urgency tingeing her words.

"How do you know which Tairseach is the original?" Alexandra asked with more concern.

"Everyone knows the Chadwick Tairseach is the original." Skyler laughed.

"Clearly not." Alexandra retorted sarcastically. "We didn't all grow up with tales of the Cosantóirí," she continued. Skyler's smile dropped, as he rubbed the back of his neck looking sheepish.

"Okay, okay. We don't have time to argue." Hector butted in. "Lexi. You designed the castles defences, so you know how they work best. I need you at the front door in charge of that." he locked eyes with Lexi and she nodded with confirmation. Lexi began to make her way from the room. "Skyler, you go with her. If they make it through that door we are going to need two of our top fighters greeting them." said Hector, patting Skyler on the shoulder in a fatherly gesture.

"We've got this." Skyler reassured the room, as he and Lexi made their way to the main door.

"Alexandra. Shura. You will stay here, in the main hall. Hopefully it won't come to it, but if it does you protect that tunnel with all you've got." Hector pointed to the corridor that led to the basement. "Malandra and I will be patrolling the hallways between the front door, and this room." he finished.

"See you on the other side, with silver masks in hand as trophies." Shura called after Hector and Malandra as they left, attempting a nonchalant tone. The door closed behind them and Shura and Alexandra stood in the silent room.

*****

A loud crackle echoed around the castle and the walls shook from an invisible impact rippling around the portal pocket. The ceiling lights swayed and flickered, and dust fell from places undisturbed for centuries, as Lexi and Skyler ran towards the main door.

"What was that?" Skyler asked unnerved. "They are breaking through the portal pocket." Lexi exclaimed, fear prickling along her skin. "How is that possible? I thought Bas couldn't enter the castle without a key?" Skyler asked, trying hard to mask his panic.

"I'm guessing she has one." Lexi replied, a crestfallen look passing across her face. Only for a moment, but Skyler noticed. He remembered that look from the hospital waiting room the night that Sascha had died. As they reached the front door Lexi slid a panel free on the wall revealing an interactive screen, one side maintained the live feed from outside of the castle, and the other could be used to control the defence system she had installed in the castle. Lexi watched on the security monitors as Bas' army continued to encroach on the castle grounds getting ever closer to the entrance. Her and Skyler were stunned as Bas launched ripples of portal power at the castle.

"How? That's not possible." Skyler replied dumbfounded, not able to believe what he was seeing.

"She has found a way to harness the portals power and use it as a weapon. Look." Lexi pointed to the screen, they both watched with horror as the portal pocket began to crumble from the onslaught of hits.

"This technology was made centuries ago, it was not built to withstand this kind of attack. And now that Bas has Sascha's key, these castle walls can no longer protect us either." she continued, vexed by what she was watching.

"I guess it's time to show them what we've got up our castle turrets." Skyler grinned mischievously.

"I guess so." said Lexi, squaring her shoulders and typing furiously on the computer screen. She had upgraded the screen in the castle wall the day they all moved in to Éan and Claw, along with its interconnected security system designed by her company. The perks of being the boss she thought to herself. Lexi tapped a large green button on the screen, the sound of cogs grating against one another and turning reverberated through the floor, and then a loud splash of liquid as the old style defences dumped copious amounts of oil around the castle. The floors would be slick and difficult to tackle, giving the Cosantóirí more time to prepare. Lexi pressed the button again and heat seeking arrows whistled from the castles arrow-slits hunting down the masked intruders as they reached the castle walls. Skyler and Lexi watched as arrows buried themselves into a handful of Bas' army, they hit the ground limp and unmoving.

"Five down. About twelve to go." Skyler muttered excitedly like he was playing on a games console. Lexi rolled her eyes at his jovial demeanour in the heat of battle, still inputting figures and instructions into the security system.

"Are you ready?" Lexi asked.

"For what?" Skyler replied, intrigued.

"For this!" Lexi pressed another button and fire erupted around the castle, licking at the oil as it went. It created a protective ring of fire, and stopped Bas in her tracks. The flames reflected on their masks, burning bright and strong in the fading light. The dancing flames caught some of the masked trespassers off guard, leaping onto their clothes and sending them running. They looked like little fireflies, all aglow, fleeing into the dusk.

"You are quite the badass, Miss Garmund." Skyler smiled, channelling Wyatt's posh accent, and bowing in a chivalrous gesture.

"That I am." stated Lexi, a rare smile gracing her face. The smile was short lived, her face returning to serious composure as she watched Bas separate the fire with portal power. "Crap!" She exclaimed furiously. "This Hündin is really starting to get on my nerves." Lexi muttered under her breath. A thunderous crash emanated from the main door, startling Skyler and Lexi in the process.

"Shit. What was that?" Skyler cussed. Lexi pointed to the monitor revealing the remainder of Bas' army using a battering ram to breach the main door. They had been so focused on Bas, they had not noticed that a section of the group had split off in a different direction and made their way to the front entrance.

"I'm out of manoeuvres, Skyler." Lexi said in a matter of fact tone.

"It's okay, we trained for this." Skyler reassured her.

"There are five of them, and two of us. And one of those five is Bas!" Lexi pointed out.

"We have won with worse odds." said Skyler with more confidence than he felt. He started to jump up and down on the spot, swinging his arms wildly as he went.

"What are you doing?" Lexi probed, looking at Skyler as if he was an alien species, her eyebrow raised in query.

"Warming up. I don't want to pull a muscle." Skyler replied as if his behaviour was perfectly usual. Another loud crash caused the door to eek open slightly, a wedge of light spilling into the corridor. Lexi passed Skyler a metal sconce from the wall.

"Here. Take this." Lexi commanded as she readied herself for what was coming. The two of them ducked into an alcove, hiding from the intruders, hoping to build up a split second of surprise. The door faltered, crashing to the floor, creating a tidal wave of dust and debris. Bas strode through the doorway, trampling over the felled door, followed by Street and three unidentifiable figures.

"I know you're here. I can feel your fear in the air, I can taste it on my tongue. Did you really think I couldn't get around your families portal pocket, and your little magic tricks? The Garmund's aren't the only family with genius running in their veins." Bas laughed cruelly, a hauntingly sweet sound.

*****

Shura placed a protective hand on Alexandra's wrist, taking a step forward in front of her, as an earth shattering crash rushed around the castle.

"They've breached the door." Shura stated, a weird calm in her tone.

"What do we do?" Alexandra asked with concern.

"Here, help me move this in front of the door." said Shura, pointing at the large banquet table. She placed her palms on the wooden table, gesturing for Alexandra to do the same. "Push." Shura shouted, as they forced the table closer to the door. It squealed across the floor in protest, bits of wood splintering from its feet.

"What is this thing made of?" Alexandra moaned, pushing the heavy table with all her might.

"Hopefully something strong enough to keep Bas on the other side of that door," panted Shura, breathing hard from the effort of moving the hulking table.

More loud noises sang around the castle, the sounds of people being thrown and weapons being fired. Alexandra and Shura pushed the table with more urgency until it rested against the metal of the door handle. A momentary breath of relief as they readied themselves.

*****

Lexi waited for the perfect time and launched herself forward, out of the alcove, landing a striking blow to the head of one of the masked figures with the sconce. They crumpled to the floor with a groan. Lexi stepped over them ready to strike again. She lifted the sconce high above her head, and then without warning she was sailing through the air a dull pain across her abdomen. Lexi realised Bas had shot her with the portal powered gun, she landed hard on the solid ground. The room went dark.

"Lexi!" Skyler yelled, watching as Bas launched her down the corridor like a rag doll. He grimaced at the crunching sound that followed Lexi hitting the floor. Bas simply turned to walk away, as if she were bored of the whole situation. Skyler ran towards Bas, anger flaring in his green eyes.

"Deal with him." Bas commanded, pointing to two of her masked minions. She strode off down the corridor with Street by her side, as two figures rounded on Skyler. Skyler came to a halt before running straight into them, pausing to decipher his next move. The masked people were fast and they were landing strong punches, Skyler held his own as he blocked, ducked, and manoeuvred out of the path of their blows. He rolled to the side, rising to his feet just in time to get clocked across the face by someone's foot. Skyler felt the heat rush to his face, the throbbing of an already forming bruise, and blurry vision from a rattled brain. A fist landed another solid punch to his other cheek knocking Skyler to the ground, he could feel the blood inside his mouth where he had bitten his own cheek. A sharp kick, followed by another, drew the breath from Skylers lungs. He reached out to the sconce lying on the floor as he struggled to breathe. The cracking sound of his now broken ribs bounced off of the castle bricks making him feel sick. Skyler's hand wrapped around the cool metal of the sconce, he pulled it in closer, then drove the sharp end into the stomach of one of his assailants. They let out a wail of pain, silenced by the gurgling of blood in their throat. The blood spilled over the mouthpiece of the mask, looking grotesque and creepy, as the stranger collapsed to the floor in a pool of their own blood. Skyler held back the urge to throw up, clambering to get to his feet before the second masked figure could launch into the next beating. Skyler braced ready for another blow as the figure wound up for an onslaught of punches. A duff thud sounded as the figure slumped to the concrete, a furious looking Lexi stood behind him, bloodied sconce in hand, and a pained expression on her face. Blood had turned Lexi's usually mousey hair a sickening shade of crimson on one side, and her wrist was hanging limply by her side. She looked fierce and determined, and Skyler couldn't help but grin at this impressive force before him. Skyler reached across to remove the mask of the now impaled and dead figure on the floor. He needed to see who they were, otherwise the silver masks would haunt him in his sleep.

"She's just a kid." Skyler said, shocked. He suddenly realised it would not be the masks that haunted him.

"This one too." stated Lexi, holding the dented silver mask in her hand. "Must be around Raimund's age." she sounded unfazed by this fact. Skyler seemed to barely hear her, he held his hand over his mouth, as if he could hold back the torrent of emotions swirling around his skull.

"She is barely even Izzy's age, and I killed her." Skyler whispered, distraught.

"Teenager or not, she was quite willing to kill you if you had not done so." Lexi replied, certain of her stance. "Come on." she instructed gently. "We need to protect the Tairseach." Lexi insisted. A loud explosion rocked the castle walls, followed by a rush of air down the corridor. "And we need to protect our family." Lexi said more fiercely. The unusual sentimentality from Lexi, and the gust of hot air grating against his skin, had Skyler on his feet, and his head mostly back in the fight.

*****

A shock of bright light, and a powerful explosion, sent fragments of the door flying across the main hall. The heavy table skidded across the floor like it was a piece of paper. The force of the blast knocked Alexandra off of her feet, sending her sliding across the tiles. A splinter of wood had buried itself in Alexandra's bicep, causing warm blood to trickle down her arm soaking into her sleeve as it went. Shura had skilfully jumped behind a chair, which took the brunt of the explosion, and was back in a fighting stance before the smoke had cleared. Alexandra winced as she pulled the foreign body from her arm, the squelch of damaged flesh making her feel light headed. Alexandra discarded the bloody sliver of wood, forcing back the dizziness, and rising to her feet. She could feel the anger rising through her body as a familiar blue cap became visible through the smoke. Without thinking Alexandra ran at Street, grabbing up a substantial chunk of debris as a makeshift weapon. She clocked him across the face with the clump of wood, his hat flew across the room, a fact that filled Alexandra with a momentary feeling of satisfaction. But the blow didn't seem to faze him, Alexandra's moment of satisfaction was gone, as he returned her act of violence with a punch to the face. Alexandra felt her lip split open, the sting of blood bringing tears to her eyes. Two hands grabbed hold of the front of Alexandra's shirt, then her feet were no longer on the ground, she was travelling through the air, coming to a sudden and jarring stop on the battered banquet table. Street had lifted her from the ground, pinning her to the table, as if she were no heavier than a small child. The suddenness of the landing had winded Alexandra as she forced herself to breathe. Street had her pinned to the remains of the table with his forearm. Alexandra watched with horror as, across the room, Bas wrapped her hands around Shura's throat squeezing tight, Shura struggled against her, fighting for air. The colour drained from Shura's face, and her arms began to visibly weaken. Alexandra tried to free herself from Street's weight, but he was strong. She watched, unable to move, as Street slid a knife from his leather boot. He dragged the cool blade along the soft skin of Alexandra's jaw line, toying with her. He was careful not to cut her as he ran the tip of the blade down her neck, pausing just above her collar bone.

"This time no one is here to save you." Street whispered, his voice rough and gravelly.

"I don't need anyone to save me." Alexandra whispered back, her voice strained but sure. Alexandra grabbed something from the table, a metal fork, and jammed the prongs into Streets neck. He jumped back in surprise, clutching his neck. Blood seeped through his fingers in torrents as he tried, unsuccessfully, to stem the bleeding. Street dropped to his knees, panic clear in his pale eyes. Alexandra rolled from the table onto her feet, slightly unsteady, but unperturbed. She dropped the bloody fork onto the table, and ran across the main hall, ducking to avoid an object being hurled in her direction by a fading Street. Alexandra grabbed hold of Bas' arm pulling her away from Shura.

Alexandra held on to Bas' arm with a vice grip, and with her other hand she grasped the key at her throat. A flash of light engulfed them both transporting them away from the castle. Alexandra had not planned beyond freeing Shura from Bas' weight, suddenly aware that she was teleporting with the Devil herself to an unknown location. If she was watching herself as a character in a film, Alexandra knew she would be screaming at herself for being such an idiot.

Alexandra hit the ground with a thud, rolling across the wet grass until she had run out of momentum. The sky bled orange as Alexandra looked up from the ground where she lay. A second of calm washed over her, her body numb to the cuts and bruises tattooing her body. Images of Shura pale and unmoving on the floor flashed in front of her eyes shattering the calm and forcing her to move. Alexandra scrambled to a kneeling position, pausing as her body struggled to keep up with her mind. She felt a heavy smack on the back of her head, the force of the blow smashed the light bulb in her brain, turning her world dark.

CHAPTER 13

THE AROMA OF BERGAMOT wafted into Alexandra's consciousness, the usually calming scent had her nerves prickling. The smell mixed with the taste of chlorine in the air causing Alexandra to feel woozy and disorientated. Her body felt strange and distant, her hands clamped down by something rough and abrasive. Alexandra tried to move her feet, but they were held in place by something strong. Her eyes felt heavy, and her head pulsed where something solid had struck her. The events that took place at the castle swam into her mind in clouded fragments, slowly becoming clearer as the fog of her concussion faded.

"Wakey, wakey, Alexandra." Casey Ray's sickly sweet voice swam into her thoughts. Alexandra felt the girls hand brush the side of her cheek, moving a strand of hair from her face. "I made tea, I remembered your favourite of course." Casey Ray continued. She spoke as if the two of them were on a date in a cute family run cafe. Judging by the buzzing sound of pylons, and the occasional rush of water, Alexandra guessed that was not the case. Casey Ray shook Alexandra's shoulders softly, making her head loll back and forth, and then more violently. "I said wake up!" she shouted in frustration all sweetness gone from her voice.

159

Alexandra slowly opened her eyes, squinting as she tried to adjust to the light of the room. Her vision was slightly blurred, and her head felt heavy.

"No need to shout." Alexandra mocked, her voice hoarse and strained. She felt as if she had been in a desert for the last forty-eight hours. Alexandra clenched her fists in an effort to free her hands from their bindings, but a nest of thick dirty rope wrapped its way around her wrists like a python, tightening its grip with every movement. She could feel her skin becoming raw from its touch, the harsh fibres bristling against her soft flesh. Alexandra tried to kick out her feet but their halted movement confirmed their trapped status. Reams of rope wound its way around her ankles. She was trapped. Tied to this uncomfortable wooden chair.

"This seems like an awful lot of effort to get back at a one night stand." Alexandra muttered sarcastically, gesturing at her restraints with disdain. "Was it because I didn't call you back?" she goaded.

Casey Ray laughed a musical laugh, but her eyes were full of rage. She raised her hand and slapped Alexandra hard across the cheek, the noise bounced off of the walls, the force bringing tears to Alexandra's eyes.

"You think I would do all of this because of one lousy lay?" Casey Ray said furiously.

"I couldn't comment where on the scale of lousy the event sits. My memory of that night is a little hazy, but you made sure of that didn't you?" Alexandra retorted struggling to keep her tone neutral as her anger bubbled beneath the surface. She hadn't had time to process what she had learnt about that night, it brought up so many unanswered questions and ranging emotions. Alexandra felt sick at the thought of someone else being in control of her body, of someone else taking away her ability to choose for herself.

"As I recall you were willingly knocking back shots, and your willingness didn't stop there." Casey Ray smiled a cruel and demeaning smile, like she knew her verbal sucker punch had landed accurately. "I mean the fact that one of those shots was laced with a little something extra didn't seem to slow you down." Casey Ray continued, twisting the proverbial knife with joy.

She walked around the chair, stopping to stand behind Alexandra, her breath sickeningly warm on the back of Alexandra's neck. Alexandra struggled against her restraints, she wanted with all her heart to get Casey Ray as far away from her as possible, but she had no such luck. The ropes were tight, and they burnt her skin as she tried to free herself. Casey Ray leant forward placing a hand on Alexandra's knee.

"Does this bring back any memories." Casey Ray whispered into Alexandra's ear, running her hand slowly up Alexandra's inner thigh. She followed the crease of Alexandra's jeans up the zipper coming to a stop as her hand toyed with the button that fastened Alexandra's jeans.

"Stop it!" Alexandra shouted desperately.

"Oh, but that's not what you said before." Casey Ray replied in a whiny, child-like tone.

"Why are you doing this?" Alexandra asked through gritted teeth, rage building inside of her.

"Because it brings me so much happiness to see you in pain, Alexandra Chadwick. Just a little taste of what your family did to me." Casey Ray replied, flicking

Alexandra's hair petulantly as she walked around to face her. "You see, Alexandra. The Chadwick dynasty has done nothing but cause my family pain, and bloodshed. Your dear old Daddy killed my brother, and your crazy Aunt killed my Father. Yet the Cosantóirí still holds your family name in high esteem." Casey Ray's tone was a terrifyingly measured calm, especially compared to the fury dancing in her eyes. "My family gets shunned for an age old misunderstanding, but yours commits murder over and over with no consequences." she ranted as if she had practiced her spiel before.

"Your family were shunned for waging a war that killed people. And clearly you didn't learn your lesson, because you're still killing people. It's just that your army is now called a criminal organisation." Alexandra spat furiously.

"You watch your tone." Casey Ray threatened, her hand shot forward and clamped itself around Alexandra's neck dangerously. "You're in my house now, Alexandra.".

"No wonder you're so screwed up, if this is where you grew up." Alexandra stated snidely, hinting at the water damaged and crumbling concrete walls in the room, at the rusty pipes, and derelict furniture and machinery that littered the area. Casey Ray tightened her grip on Alexandra's throat, cutting of her air supply, watching as Alexandra's lips turned an unhealthy shade of blue.

"I wonder. Did anyone ever tell you that your petulant sarcasm would be the death of you?" Casey Ray mused. Alexandra's vision threatened to go dark as her body used the last of the oxygen in her lungs. Then the tightness at her throat was gone as Casey Ray released her with a laugh. "Not yet. Not yet." Casey Ray whispered to herself, as she walked off into another room. Alexandra watched as Casey Ray left the room, she waited for the door to close shut behind her, then desperately began looking for a way out. The sign on the far wall read *Water Treatment Facility*, which explained the pipes, the old metal equipment, the old remains of furniture, and the sound of rushing water, she thought to herself. A sense of dread filled her at the thought of where in the world they were, because they could literally be anywhere in the world. She was suddenly very aware of the downside to teleportation.

"Shit." she cursed through gritted teeth, frustration building as she tried and failed to loosen her bindings. Alexandra spotted an old desk across the room, bits of it looked like they had been pulled off hastily leaving rusted nails poking out on one side. Adrenaline began pumping through her veins at the glimmer of escape before her. She heaved her body right and then forced it left causing the chair to skid across the floor a little way. It rocked precariously as she tried again, and again, and again. She was making slow progress but she was almost halfway there. The sound of footsteps coming towards the room left a taste of bile in Alexandra's mouth as panic began to rise again. She closed her eyes and asked the universe to cut her a break, asking and hoping that Casey Ray would not notice the chair had moved.

"I hope you're ready for story time, because, well, I have got a good one for you." Casey Ray said cheerfully. Her changing moods were making Alexandra dizzy, but the other girl hadn't noticed Alexandra had moved across the room. Alexandra exhaled with a smidge of relief. She never imagined she would be relieved that someone was too unhinged to notice a human attached to a chair had travelled a few feet across the room. "It's all about this sweet, pretty blonde." Casey Ray paused for affect, tossing her blonde hair behind one shoulder. "That's me." Casey Ray winked. "This sweet little blonde, she joins a quaint little book club hosted by a kooky older lady." Casey Ray smiled cruelly as she watched Alexandra's face drop with realisation. "Yes. You guessed it. That kooky lady is Alondra Chadwick. That crazy bat let me right into her home every week for a year. You see I'm patient like that, I can drag these things out for as long as I want. I like to make sure when I strike, it's a perfect. Kill. Shot." Casey Ray poked Alexandra in the centre of her forehead with her finger to enunciate her words. Alexandra could feel her skin prickling with anger, and she pictured letting that rage fly free when she was no longer tied to this rotting chair. Casey Ray moved in closer until their noses were almost touching, Alexandra instinctively tried to move her head back, but Casey Ray grabbed a handful of Alexandra's hair and held her head in place. Alexandra could feel strands of her hair being tugged from her scalp.

"Do you want to know what the nice little blonde did next? I'm certain that you do. The blonde turned up early to book club one week and, before the crazy old lady had time to realise, she plunged a dagger into her stomach." Casey Ray tilted her head to the side curiously, watching Alexandra's eyes fill with tears. "This dagger to be specific." Casey Ray revealed, brandishing the ornate silver dagger in her free hand. She brought the shining blade up to Alexandra's neck, flicking it quickly she nicked her soft skin. Alexandra flinched at the sting of the cool blade, watching with revulsion as Casey Ray licked a drop of blood from the knife's edge.

164

"The girl watched as the life left the old woman's body, and revelled at the Chadwick blood soaking into the floor. She thought how just it was. Blood for blood and all that. The end." Casey Ray sounded almost gleeful, and she was beaming from ear to ear.

Alexandra was shaking with hatred and pain, a feeling so powerful, and one she had never felt about another human before. To Casey Ray's surprise Alexandra flung her head forward, crashing into Casey Ray's nose with a sickening crack. The girl screamed in pain and staggered backwards. Blood streamed from Casey Ray's nose, staining her hands, and the floor at her feet, with its volume.

"You bitch!" Casey Ray spat, blood smeared on her teeth.

"I always say never go for the head butt. But I have to admit it is highly satisfying in this situation." Alexandra smirked with satisfaction, mildly aware that she was about to pay for her momentary loss of control.

CHAPTER 14

"ALEXANDRA!" SHURA YELLED HELPLESSLY, watching as the rippling air swallowed Alexandra and Bas up. She clutched her throat, it felt bruised and sore, but she was grateful to be taking in air once again. "Shit!" she cursed, slapping the floor with her palm in frustration. Shura looked around the room, taking in the carnage surrounding her; Street dead in a crumpled mess on the floor, furniture strewn in pieces around the room, and splinters of wood and metal embedded in the walls resembling blood splatter in their appearance.

"Shura! Alexandra!" Skyler's voice echoed from the corridor. He sounded panic stricken and overwhelmed. Shura tried to get to her feet, but her body had other plans, and she collapsed back to the spot where she started from. She felt tired and weak, like she could happily sleep for the next year.

Alexandra's smiling face, in her crimson red dress, floated into her thoughts. In that moment Shura realised she didn't have time to sit, she didn't have time to fall apart, that could happen later. Right now she needed to find Alexandra. Shura had never imagined that another human could affect her in this way, but Alexandra had scaled her walls and fought off her defences, and now, even after such a short time, she couldn't imagine a world without her raven curls.

"Shura? Oh god, Shura." Skyler vaulted over a segment of the destroyed table and ran towards his sister. Skyler looked like he had gone ten rounds against Nicola Adams, his face was one big bruise. His green eyes were filled with tears, and panic painted his face. Lexi was only seconds behind him, she avoided the table and dashed through the middle to stand with the siblings. She looked bloodied and bruised, but still managed to stand with a poise that said she could take on the world and win. Shura had to admit she admired that about Lexi, her sheer force of will and her unshakeable confidence.

"I'm okay. I'm okay." Shura protested as Skyler began to fuss around her. "I feel like I fared better than the two of you. What happened? You both look like hell. No offense." she continued, trying to hide her concern with humour.

"Where is Alexandra?" Lexi asked, ignoring Shura's comments.

"She portalled out of here with Bas." Shura said, her eyes welling with fear and anger.

"What do you mean?" Skyler asked, as if one more piece of bad news might tip him over the edge.

"I mean, Alexandra saved my life and portalled that psycho, Bas, out of here. But she never came back." Shura's voice rose in anger, her eyes shining as she forced back tears.

"Bas has Alexandra?" Malandra asked with concern as she entered the room. She was covered in dirt and dust, her hair now housing fragments of debris. She scanned the room, her eyes slightly wild. "Where is Hector? And Raimund and Izzy?" Malandra panicked.

"I believe Raimund and Izzy are still safely with the Tairseach. As for Hector, we have not seen him since we all parted for our stations." Lexi answered seemingly unfazed, and calm.

"He was supposed to be with you." Shura stated.

"He was. But then an explosion of some sort brought down a section of the ceiling, and when I came to, he was gone." Malandra looked close to tears. The sadness in her eyes was unfamiliar in someone so often full of joy.

"What do you mean gone?" Skyler asked, his frazzled brain and battered body struggling to keep up.

"I mean, gone. I've searched the whole castle, and I can't find Hector anywhere." Malandra replied heartbroken.

"Perhaps Hector is simply looking for all of us too. So let us deal with one problem at a time." Lexi reasoned with the room. "Skyler I need you to check on Raimund and Izzy, bring them to meet us in the infirmary. Malandra I need you to pull it together, you're our medic and we all need you." she gestured at her own limp arm, and Shura's bruised throat.

"But what about Alexandra? And Hector? We need to find them." Shura implored.

Lexi could see the emotions swimming in Shura's eyes, she could see how much the girl cared for Alexandra, she had felt those same feelings many times over the years.

"Lexi is right. We are no use to them battered and broken." Malandra agreed, surprising the room as she aligned with Lexi.

Lexi reached out her hand to Shura, an olive branch of friendship, and pulled her to a standing position. Lexi hoped that Shura could see, in her eyes, that she understood her feelings, that she could pass on a sort of silent comfort with a simple look.

*****

Shura despised the sterile brightness of the white infirmary, it was too clean, too white, too clinical. She understood the reasoning behind all of these things, but it still made her feel far from calm and relaxed.

"Hold still." Malandra urged Lexi.

"Easy to say when you are not the one with a broken wrist." Lexi retorted coldly.

"I offered you pain meds. You said they would cloud your judgment." Malandra replied with frustration. Malandra held Lexi's wrist firmly then with a fast pull and twist, and a disgusting crack, she nodded proudly. "There. It's back in-line." she spoke calmly. Lexi looked like she was holding back numerous expletives, and the urge to punch the other woman in the face, the restraint made her face redden and her neck vein pulse. Malandra wrapped the severely bruised wrist in soft clean bandages, placing a support over the top. "We don't have time to make an actual cast. So this will have to do for now." She smiled, attempting to be reassuring.

"It's fine. It is actually less uncomfortable now." Lexi admitted, the redness in her cheeks calming to a subtle blush.

"Good, I'm glad." Malandra said with genuine kindness. "I do also need to place some stitches on that nasty looking head wound of yours.".

"That will take up too much time. Just glue it together for now." Lexi ordered, to Malandra's chagrin. "I think I might have a way to track Alexandra and Hector. Or at least their Tairseach key." said Lexi, ignoring Malandra's attempt to protest.

"Of course you do." Shura snarked, tiredness threatening to engulf her. She was sat on the edge of the cotton bed, pulling slithers of wood and debris from her shoulder. Shura dropped the tweezers onto the metal tray with a clatter. "What's your idea?" she asked in a more neutral tone, placing a sterile dressing over her bloodied shoulder.

"Well. I have been developing new tracking technology." Lexi continued, immune to Shura's sarcasm by now. "I had hoped it would be useful in tracking Bas, so we could be at least one step ahead of her. But I am sure I can recalibrate it to track Alexandra and Hector. I have both the Chadwick and the Sarkis Tairseach frequency already, in theory I should be able to use that to find them." Lexi sounded hopeful as she explained her idea.

"That sounds like a great idea Lexi." Izzy's sweet tone floated into the room. Followed by a gaunt looking Skyler being half carried by Raimund. "I think Skyler requires your help, Malandra. He is not looking so hot, as the Americans say on the television." she looked pleased at her popular culture reference, and was rewarded by a chuckle from Malandra and a grin from Skyler.

"The adrenaline must have faded." Raimund said with concern. "He began getting worse on our way up to you." he continued, placing Skyler on the closest free bed.

*****

"Malandra! Malandra can you hear me?" Hector yelled down the corridor to no response. His own voice simply echoed back, as if it had bounced off of an invisible wall. He touched his hand to his throbbing forehead, concerned at the searing pain travelling from one temple to the other. To his relief his hand came away free of blood. *What is going on?* Hector muttered to himself. The last thing he could recall was a loud explosion, followed by the ceiling crumbling in, then he was here in this corridor. It looked the same as the corridor he had been standing in before the explosion, but the walls and ceilings were completely intact here. Hector couldn't explain it, the castle felt the same but something was not quite right about it. There was something odd, and different about this place. It didn't feel like Éan and Claw. As he inspected the walls more closely they rippled slightly, as if they were an illusion in his mind. A wave of panic set in at the thought that maybe he was trapped inside his own mind, maybe he was in a coma, or maybe he had not survived the blast and now he was doomed to walk the halls of the castle forever. In his spiral of panic Hector didn't see the uneven cobble sticking up at his feet. His shoe caught on the stone and he tripped, his knees hit the ground and his hand grazed the wall. Hector could feel the tingling of grazed flesh on his hand. He smiled, sitting up against the wall, as he inspected his hand. Imaginary men don't bleed, and dead men certainly don't he thought to himself, panic subsiding momentarily.

*****

"So what exactly is your plan to find Hector and Alexandra?" Skyler asked again as he lay sprawled on the infirmary bed covered in bandages and stitches. There was barely an inch of him that wasn't covered in a bruise, or cut, or broken bone. Skyler looked dazed and confused, and Malandra was staring at him with concern.

"I have developed some software that can search for specific frequencies. And since each key runs on the same frequency as its respective Tairseach, I can put Hector and Alexandra's Tairseach frequencies into the algorithm to find their keys. And in turn find them." Lexi repeated proudly.

"Let's just hope they both still have their keys on them then." Shura said, unconvinced at the likely success of Lexi's plan.

"I brought your laptop Lexi." Izzy announced as she danced into the room, laptop in hand.

"Thank you Izzy. Once I input the data it shouldn't take long to find them. I suggest we split into teams to increase our efficiency." Lexi stated, already typing furiously on the keyboard. "Raimund, Izzy. You two can be in charge of the search for Hector, whilst Shura and I find Alexandra." she continued without pausing.

"What about me? I can help." Skyler protested, shifting uncomfortably in the bed.

"I think it's best if you stay here, Skyler. We need you recovered." Lexi replied, not fully paying attention.

"Malandra you should stay too. In case of any medical emergencies."

"Yes boss." Malandra responded, fighting the urge to protest out of principle. She didn't like being told what to do, even if she knew it was the right call.

"I've narrowed it down to this old water treatment facility in Southern California." Lexi announced, pointing at a map on the screen.

"Then let's go." said Shura impatiently.

"We cannot just go barrelling in there, we need a plan." Lexi retorted.

"Portal in, grab A.C, portal out. There, plan made. Now let's go." Shura snarked.

*****

The birds were singing in the trees, the sun shining through their branches in beams of warmth. Alexandra smiled at the pleasant smell of the forest, the blooming flowers filling her path with bright purples, yellows, and oranges, as she wandered down the pathway. She could feel a hand in her own, and she felt calm and safe, Alexandra looked up to see Shura's cheeky grin staring back at her. A purple flower was nestled in her messy blonde hair, vibrant in the summer light. She could stay here forever, Alexandra thought to herself, she felt so happy and at home here. But where was *here*? It looked like the forest on the Chadwick grounds, but it smelled different, and the path was going the wrong way through the trees. Dark clouds began to rumble into the skies, covering the warm sun. Alexandra shivered, her hand no longer comforted by another, she was cold and alone in the forest. She could feel her heart pounding, her breathing felt laboured, and her head hurt. The smell of chemicals wafted into the forest, and she could hear pylons buzzing above her. Alexandra tried to move, but she was stuck, like a stick in the mud. The smell of chlorine was getting stronger, and suddenly the forest was gone. It's happiness and safety replaced with pain and fear. Alexandra could feel something warm dripping down her cheek, and her fingers felt disconnected from her hand. She struggled to open her eyes, they felt bruised and uncomfortable. Alexandra managed to focus long enough to confirm her right hand and two fingers were broken, and that blood oozed from her thigh where a knife had once been. She shut her eyes quickly, hoping she could stop this new reality from entering the forest. But Alexandra had no such luck. The intensity of the chlorine in the room made her cough, causing a ripple effect of pain to run across her body highlighting where she was bruised and broken. The realisation that if she didn't get out she would likely die here, caused a surge of determination and enough adrenaline to mask some of the pain.

I refuse to die in this disgusting room, tied to this musty old chair. Alexandra mumbled to the universe, blood spraying from her split lip as she spoke. She mustered up all the strength left in her body, and launched the chair towards the table, then again, and again. Finally, Alexandra skidded into the path of the rusty nails, just avoiding being impaled by them. She worked her wrist up and down, moving the rope against the sharp point of the nail. It felt like an age before the rope began to fray, Alexandra kept going, looking around every now and then to ensure Casey Ray wasn't lurking somewhere. Alexandra pulled at the final thread, it burnt against her skin, but finally the stubborn rope let go of her wrist. She rushed to untie her other arm, fumbling over the knots, then reached to free her trapped ankles. Alexandra kicked one foot out, and then the other, the air grazing gently across her raw skin as she stepped unsteadily away from the chair. Alexandra's legs buckled slightly, and she clung to the desk for support, as her body tried to remember how to move. A subtle humming filled her ears, accompanied by the familiar vibration of her Tairseach key. She reached up to her throat, but her key was not there. Following her connection to the key she spotted it the other side of the room, hanging on an old nail by the door. Alexandra was so focused on the key she didn't notice Casey Ray in the doorway.

"Aren't you a clever one." Casey Ray's southern twang echoed around the room. The sound of her voice making Alexandra nauseous. "But I hope you don't think you're going anywhere. I'm not done with you yet." she said with malice. She strode towards Alexandra, a fire of fury burning in her eyes. Alexandra tried to run, to make it to the door, but her legs were too unstable and she stumbled. Casey Ray grabbed a handful of Alexandra's hair and flung her backwards by her curls. Alexandra hit the back wall, slumping to the floor next to the desk. Alexandra wasn't sure how much more her body could take, but she pulled herself to her feet anyway. She could feel herself swaying as she tried to take a fighting stance, waves of dizzying pain ebbing too and throw pushing her like she was the sand at the shoreline. Alexandra watched as the air in front of her rippled with energy, taking on a life of its own and creating a protective barrier between herself and Casey Ray. The familiar musty castle smell of Éan and Claw filled the room, a scent that made Alexandra feel oddly safe. Two shadows appeared out of the disturbed air as if painted by magic. Alexandra blinked furiously trying to determine if the shadows were friend or foe, imagination or reality.

*****

The colours seemed to pass by more slowly than usual in the portal, Shura felt as if she was portalling in slow motion. She was terrified about what they might find at the other end, perhaps her brain was slowing everything down to prepare her she thought. Shura just wanted to get there, she wanted to find A.C., she wanted her to be safe. But just like when you're on an eight hour flight, to explore an exciting new city, time seems to stutter and slow. She couldn't stop thinking about how long Bas had been holding A.C., and her mind kept taking her to all the worst case scenarios. Shura shook her head, actively trying to shake the thoughts from her mind, to focus on what was coming. A subtle buzzing sound thrummed its way into the portal, the sound of electric lines or pylons. Then a strange aroma of damp and bergamot engulfed Shura like a cloud. She could taste chlorine in the air, the warmth in the portal intensifying it. Then her feet hit ground. She landed sure and steady, raising her head to take in her surroundings. Lexi had landed beside her, barely a second behind, and she was poised and ready for anything. Shura could see anger flash across Lexi's face, only a momentary drop in composure but Shura clocked it. She followed Lexi's eye line to discern the cause of her rage, and she locked eyes with Bas. The girl looked surprised by their appearance, a look that quickly turned to annoyance and disdain. Shura had no time for Bas, she came for Alexandra. She scanned the room desperately searching for the signature raven curls she had come to adore. "A.C!" Shura shouted with concern as she spotted Alexandra swaying precariously at the back of the room.

*****

"Are you certain that this is where Lexi pinpointed Hectors Tairseach key?" Raimund asked, his arms outstretched in query at the rubble filled, but empty, corridor.

"Yes, she showed me on the laptop." Izzy replied, hopping between chunks of rubble and peering underneath spaces big enough to hide a person.

"I'm almost certain Hector is not hiding under there." Raimund goaded.

"I am looking for the key, silly." Izzy jested back. She continued to jump around the debris as if she were in a concrete jungle.

"Of course." Raimund replied simply. He admired her free spirit, and her joy. Raimund often wished he could go back to a place where he was that care-free, that innocent, that happy. But too much had happened to go back to that place for him, though he hoped that maybe one day he could go forward to a place of happiness. It did feel like he was finally getting his life back on track, Raimund had been clean and sober for almost three weeks. He smiled to himself, and for the first time in a long time he felt proud of himself. This was the longest time he had spent clean since his brother's death, and it felt good. It was hard, and he had to work at it constantly, but he was beating it, the voice that told him he needed the drug, he was beating it.

"Did you hear that?" Izzy asked. "That vibration. It sounds familiar.".

"I hear it too. It's the same noise I hear when I travel via Tairseach." Raimund explained, a hint of confusion in his voice.

*****

"Raimund? Raimund can you hear me?" Hector shouted. He could hear Raimund's dry tone, almost as if they were in the same room. Yet his corridor still remained empty.

"Izzy?" He yelled, as her musical tone danced around the hallway. What a strange sensation it was to hear the voices of your loved ones, but to not be able to see them or communicate back. This is not how he imagined it, when he thought about the afterlife. Though Hector knew that's not what this was, he was in the in-between, not quite in the real world with everyone else, and not so far beyond that he couldn't come back (or at least he hoped not). Hector followed the echo of voices to where they were loudest, placing his palm on the invisible barrier that held him in this corridor.

"Raimund. Izzy." He bellowed again, banging on the clear wall like a mime. Hector paused, then knocked again, and again, the noise rippling around him in a wave. He recognised that sound, he'd been listening to it for the past fifty years, it was the sound that used to scare him but that he now found comforting. The noise accompanied him on every trip through the Tairseach - it was the sound of portal power. Hector relaxed his shoulders slightly, the Cosantóirí were connected to the portal power, the others would sense it. If they could feel the portal power, then they could find him, and he wouldn't be stuck in the in-between.

CHAPTER 15

ALEXANDRA BREATHED A SIGH of relief at Shura's familiar voice, her legs collapsing as her body gave into the pain and the tiredness. Shura ran to her, placing a comforting hand delicately on Alexandra's cheek. Shura's eyes welled with tears, her face grave. In that moment Alexandra realised how hurt she must look. Bloodied, bruised, and broken clinging to a destroyed desk for support. Shura's eyes blazed with anger as she clocked Alexandra's broken hand, and the blood oozing from her thigh wound. She placed a gentle kiss on Alexandra's forehead, a gesture full of love and kindness.

"Stay here." Shura whispered. Then without warning she whirled around to face Bas. Shura could feel her searing temper burning like adrenaline around her body. "Lexi, get A.C. back to Éan and Claw." she ordered, trying to keep her tone level.

"If you think that I am going to leave you on your own to slay a monster, you are very mistaken Shura." Lexi argued back.

"Just do it." Shura shouted. "Please," she continued in a softer tone, pleading as she turned to look at Lexi. "Please. I have got this." Shura reassured Lexi, who looked like she was going through a serious internal struggle as to the best course of action. Shura watched as

Lexi gazed at her broken wrist, and then back to Alexandra who was barely conscious in the corner. She watched as the decision clarified itself in Lexi's mind, her face set and stoic as she nodded in agreement.

"We will see you shortly." Lexi stated, not usually one for sentiment. She rushed over to Alexandra, looping the girls arm around her shoulder, and heaving her to her feet. Lexi grasped the key at her neck, the air rippled around them and swallowed them up.

****

Lexi just about managed to stay on her feet, holding onto a limp Alexandra, as they hit the dusty floor of Éan and Claw. They had arrived in front of the infirmary door, to Lexi's relief. She was not sure if she could carry Alexandra much further, the last few days had really zapped her of energy and strength. The sound of hurried footsteps came from inside the infirmary, followed by the creak of the door swinging open revealing Malandra standing in the doorway. Malandra's face dropped at the sight of Alexandra, barely conscious and bleeding onto the concrete floor. The vibrant red of the blood stood out dramatically against the dusty grey of the floor.

"Let's get her to the nearest bed." Malandra ordered with urgency.

"Where is Shura. Where is my sister?" Skyler demanded. He grimaced as he tried to readjust his position on the bed.

"She stayed behind." Lexi said hesitantly as she helped lift Alexandra onto the bed.

"You left her with Bas?" Skyler accused.

"No." Lexi retorted angrily. "Shura asked me to go, to keep Alexandra safe. So I did. You don't get to accuse me from your bed, you weren't there.".

"Lexi." Malandra chided. Alexandra moaned in pain, bringing the room back to its senses.

"Is Alexandra going to be okay?" Skyler asked, his words full of guilt over not having asked sooner.

"She is in very capable hands." stated Lexi. Both Skyler and Malandra looked at her with surprise.

"Are you okay?" Skyler jested. "I mean I think you just complemented Malandra." he grinned cheekily.

"I think the focus should be on Alexandra, don't you agree." Lexi replied.

"Lexi is clearly fine." Malandra chuckled. "But she is also correct. I am going to need a suture kit, and I want an x-ray of that hand too." she continued in a more serious tone, turning back to inspect Alexandra's injuries. "Is the portable CT machine you developed up and running yet, because I need that now. She has a lot of facial bruising and I don't want to miss anything." Malandra spoke directly to Lexi, who nodded and collected the equipment she needed.

*****

Shura watched as Lexi and Alexandra were engulfed by the air around them. She took in a steadying breath then turned her attentions back to Bas, who looked oddly bemused. They stood in silence for an uncomfortable moment, in the middle of the old water treatment control room. Remains of desks, railings, pipes, and hardware filled the dank room. The smell of chlorine so present and overwhelming in the air that it caught in your throat, threatening to choke you.

"I have to admit I wasn't expecting the cavalry so soon. I had so much more fun planned." Casey Ray whined, her tone like that of a needy toddler. "On a side note, Alexandra certainly has a type." she smirked, scanning Shura curiously with her eyes as if she were about to give her a mark out of ten for her fashion sense.

"I wouldn't call it a type. You see she chose me. But you had to drug her to be her type." said Shura trying to maintain her composure. She could see the fury in Casey Ray's eyes at the comment, Shura had successfully hit a nerve. As quickly as the rage appeared it was gone from the other woman's face, replaced by a sickening smirk and an out of place laugh. Casey Ray began to walk around the edge of the room, running her fingers along the rusted water pipes. Her forced calm was a terrifying scene to behold.

"Isn't it funny how these pipes, this building, used to be the heart of a whole city. Pumping life into the people who lived here. Then one day, when the people moved on, this building became obsolete, forgotten about, and left to rot. You see people are fickle things, and when something, or someone, is no longer of use to them. Well. You end up obsolete, forgotten, and left to rot." Casey Ray lectured. "So when Alexandra no longer has use for you. Obsolete. Forgotten. Left to rot." she smiled cruelly.

"It makes me almost feel bad for you, that you feel that way." Shura mocked. "It makes me think that really you are the one who is obsolete, the one who people forget, and the one who was left to rot." she continued. "I have to wonder, who you were before you were left to

183

rot into the heartless shell of a human you are today."
Shura mused. Casey Ray stopped in her tracks, the veins
in her neck stood out and her jaw was set, Shura could tell
she had pushed the right button this time. Casey Ray
clenched her fist around a metal object - a wrench - from
on top of the old pipes. She spun around and launched
the wrench towards Shura, but Shura was prepared for it.
She ducked and rolled to the side, landing in a crouch
ready for the next projectile, the wrench clattered to the
floor behind her just missing her head.

"I'm gonna make sure you never forget me." Casey Ray
spat, as she ran at Shura. Casey Ray slammed Shura into
the wall behind her, swinging to punch her in the face.
Shura moved her head, and the crunch of knuckles
against concrete reverberated along the wall. Casey Ray let
out a cry of pain, and Shura pushed the other woman
away from her. Shura grasped her Tairseach key just long
enough to portal behind Casey Ray, she retrieved the
wrench and swung it, landing a blow to Casey Ray's head.
She hit the ground, blood trickling from the wound.
Casey Ray simply laughed, an unhinged and hysterical
laugh.

"Clever. Very clever. Did Hector teach you that little
trick?" She rasped. She kicked out her feet surprising
Shura as she wiped her legs out from under her. Shura
landed on her back, her head making contact with the
concrete. Casey Ray forced herself into a standing
position, looking down at Shura dazed on the floor. "I
taught myself that trick." She said snidely. Casey Ray
kicked Shura in the stomach, again and again. Shura
gasped as if all of the air had been forced from her lungs.
She reached for the Tairseach key once more, and

portalled to the other side of the room, Shura landed in an uncomfortable heap on the ground. Taking in deep breaths she steadied herself, easing herself up into a kneeling position, then eventually to her feet. Casey Ray looked like she might explode with the rage she was trying to contain.

"You know what I just don't understand. You are a smart woman, you could have done anything with your talents, been anything, you could have changed the world for the better. Just imagine what you could have achieved if you channelled all of this energy into something positive. But instead you chose this path. You chose revenge. You chose to live in the bitterness, and the hatred and it turned you into this." Shura gestured at Casey Ray, stood covered in her own blood.

"I chose family, and legacy, and if you're telling me you wouldn't make the same choice then you're a liar." Casey Ray retorted angrily.

"I am nothing like you. I would never make the choices that you have." Shura shot back.

"But you already did Shura. You made that choice today when you sent Lexi and Alexandra away. You chose revenge in that moment. It's the same reason you haven't portalled out of here yourself. Isn't it?" Casey Ray grinned triumphantly.

Shura laughed incredulously. "Yes, I chose family. But my decision was made from a place of love, to protect. Your decisions come from selfishness and pride. They come from the need to be remembered no matter the cost. You cloak your actions in talk about your family, and how they were slighted, about how everyone else is to blame for your bad life." Shura continued.

"They are to blame. The Cosantóirí made me who I am." Casey Ray bellowed back.

"No." Shura yelled. "You are who you are because of your own choices, your own actions.".

Casey Ray let out an otherworldly scream, filled with all of her pent up rage, hatred, and hurt.

"You're wrong." she yelled as she ran at Shura. Shura reached for a broken piece of wood atop the desk she had landed next to. She held it out like a spear just as Casey Ray was within touching distance. The girl ran straight into the makeshift spear, impaling herself in the side. The shock was clear on Casey Ray's face, as she looked down to the bloody mess around the wooden object. Shura let go of the weapon, and watched as Casey Ray took a few stumbling steps backwards. Casey Ray laughed, a manic and strange laugh, blood staining her teeth as she coughed up her own blood. The air began to ripple and change around Casey Ray, until all that was left was her haunting laugh and a spray of blood on the floor. Shura took a step forward, nervously waiting for her to reappear, but she did not. Bas was gone. Shura took a moment to collect herself, had she just killed Bas. Surely no-one could survive being impaled in the gut. She wiped her hands through her messy hair, as she slid to the floor. Her whole body ached, and her ribs felt like they were on fire. Uncontrollable sobs took over her body, a sign of relief that she was still alive, a sign of pain, and a hint of sadness. Shura let the tears take over until there were no more to come. How sad it was that someone could be so riddled with hatred, and so moulded by anger that it ruled their every decision, it encircled their every choice. It must be so lonely for a soul to live in the darkness, completely abandoned by the light. Shura understood how easy it was to fall prey to anger and hurt, but how much stronger it made you to learn to forgive and embrace the light. She knew how hard it was to let go of the rage, she had struggled when her mother had died, when her father had died, and she was still struggling after Sascha's death. There was a constant battle between the dark and the light, and some days one can be more triumphant than the other, but she would never wish for that fighting to cease, because one cannot thrive without the humbling of the other.

A glint of something shiny caught Shura's attention, piercing through her tears, as she raised her head. Shura struggled to her feet, guided by the sparkle from across the room, and as she looked more closely a small delicate key came into focus. She recognised the shiny chain and the grubby key, they usually sat comfortably around Alexandra's neck. She retrieved the Tairseach key, wiping a smear of blood from its surface as she cradled it in her hand. Then Shura wiped her face, placed Alexandra's key in her pocket, and clutched her own Tairseach key.

"Take me home. Take me to Éan and Claw." Shura whispered.

The temperature in the portal was comforting like a warm hug carrying her home, it reminded her of being a child. Of when she would fall asleep in the car and her Dad would carry her carefully and quietly to her room. How he would place her under the covers, tuck her in, and give her a delicate kiss on the forehead. Shura smiled at the memory. The smell of the castle wafted into the portal as she gently touched down in the corridor. The stale smell of old books, and old building, had become oddly comforting too. Maybe she was just grateful to be anywhere that didn't taste like chlorine. Shura walked down the corridor, heading for the infirmary, she was fairly certain that was where everyone would be. The Cosantóirí had taken a beating in the last twenty four hours. She got to the infirmary door, and paused. What if there was more bad news waiting for her in there, she thought. Shura closed her eyes, collected her thoughts, and tentatively opened the door.

"How is everyone?" Shura asked as she stepped gingerly into the infirmary. "How is A.C?".

"Shura! We have been so worried about you." said Malandra, embracing Shura in a hug. She eased off the hug as Shura tensed in pain.

"Are you okay?" Skyler called from across the room, an edge of desperation mixed with relief in his voice. He looked like a little school boy trying to peer over a crowd of tall people, as he bobbed and weaved his head to get a glimpse of Shura, just to confirm she was in one piece.

"I'm okay." Shura reassured her brother. "I'm okay." she said again to Malandra, who was looking at her with concern. Inspecting her bruised cheek, and the way Shura was holding her side, as if she knew what injuries she had without actually seeing them.

"And Bas?" Lexi asked.

"Bas is gone." Shura stated simply, too worn out to go into details. "How is Alexandra?" she asked again.

CHAPTER 16

ALEXANDRA'S BODY FELT HEAVY as she lay between the soft infirmary sheets. She could hear voices chattering around her, but her eyes were not ready to open yet. She drifted back into her dream world. She was running around the gardens at Chadwick Manor. Alexandra's giggle echoed back at her as her Dad chased her around the grounds. Her bare feet felt cool against the blades of grass as she ran, and danced, and played. She felt so full of happiness as her Dad scooped her up, he cradled her, and carried her back to the picnic blanket by the flowers. Alexandra's Mum was waiting for them, her arms outstretched and a smile so big and glorious on her face. Alexandra didn't want to leave this place, it was so carefree, so happy, so peaceful. Her body did not hurt here, no one was hunting her and her friends here, life was so simple just playing in the grass.

"You cannot stay here sweetheart. There are people waiting for you." Mrs. Chadwick said calmly to her daughter.

"But I want to stay with you and Dad. I've missed you both so much." Alexandra sobbed.

"We know, Alexandra. We have missed you too. But we are still with you. In your memories, in your dreams, we follow you in your heart." Mr. Chadwick said softly.

"We are so very proud of you, Alexandra." Mrs. Chadwick smiled. "You need to open your eyes. Open your eyes Alexandra.".

"Just open your eyes Alexandra." Shura's voice sang into her dreams. She sounded so sad, it made Alexandra's heart stutter for a second. Her parents were right, there were people waiting for her, people she truly cared for. Alexandra's eyes fluttered open, tears rolling slowly to the bed sheets beneath her. She smiled at the vibrant green eyes staring back at her.

*****

"I am going to check-in with Raimund and Izzy. They must have found Hector by now." Lexi whispered to Malandra as they watched Alexandra and Shura from the doorway. She placed a comforting hand on Malandra's shoulder, a sign of friendship and understanding, before heading off to find the others. Lexi walked slowly down the corridor taking in the silence, it was a welcome relief. It reminded her of walking through Hamburg early in the morning, when the streets were just waking up. The streets were so empty when the sun was rising, it was clean, quiet, and so beautiful as the light bathed the empty city. In this moment the candle light bathed the corridor, in its silent and empty beauty. Lexi rounded the corner to see Raimund and Izzy staring intently at an empty corridor. They seemed to be listening for something.

"What are the two of you doing?" Lexi asked. Izzy and Raimund turned around startled by her presence.

"Lexi!" Izzy said with glee. "You are back." she ran to, and embraced Lexi in a warm hug. Lexi patted Izzy gently, she wasn't really a hugger, but she was grateful for the sentiment all the same. "Did you bring Alexandra home?" Izzy asked hopefully.

"Yes. Malandra is looking after her now." Lexi reassured them both.

"We have found Hector. We think." Raimund explained. Lexi looked perplexed as she took in the empty corridor once more. Raimund followed her gaze until her eyes looked back to him with disbelief. "Just hear us out." Raimund asked.

"Listen." Izzy requested with a smile. "Do you hear it?".

"I don't hear anything." Lexi replied.

"Listen closer." Raimund pleaded. As if on cue, the vibrations rolled down the corridor one at a time.

"It sounds like portal power vibrations." Lexi said in awe. "But how?" she asked intrigued.

"That is the part we haven't figured out yet." Raimund replied. "But we think Hector is trapped inside a portal." he continued. Raimund watched as Lexi began to tap in sequence on the castle wall. "What are you doing?" he asked.

"Trying to communicate with Hector. He knows Morse code, so if he is trapped we can talk to him." Lexi explained as she continued to tap away.

"You know Morse code? Who am I kidding, of course you do." said Raimund both impressed and unsurprised. He stood in amazement as she tapped against the wall.

"Dot, dot, dot, dot. Dot. Dash, dot, dash, dot. Dash. Dash, dash, dash. Dot, dash, dot." Lexi tapped away on the wall. "H-e-c-t-o-r." Lexi explained to a perplexed Raimund and Izzy.

"Dash, dot, dash, dash. Dot. Dot, dot, dot." Hector sounded back.

"Y-e-s." Lexi translated. "He is here." she said, shocked. "Hector, can you find a way out of the portal?" she called out.

"Dash, dot. Dash, dash, dash." Hector tapped in reply.

"What did he say?" Raimund said, intrigued.
Lexi let her head drop slightly, and her face looked sad.

"He said, no. He has no way out of the portal." she said in a quiet voice.

"Don't worry Hector, we will find a way to get you out of there." Izzy promised.

"Will we?" Raimund asked, unsure.

"We will." Lexi replied, though her words sounded more confident than her face looked.

*****

"Hey, pretty lady. Welcome back to the land of the living." Shura spoke softly, a smile playing at the corners of her mouth. Her hand was laced through Alexandra's, and the other held onto her arm. Shura looked like she was scared to let go, in case Alexandra disappeared. As though holding on to her could protect her, keep her safe.

Alexandra couldn't help but smile back, and she squeezed Shura's hand in response.

"Hey, yourself. Glad to see you're in one piece." Alexandra replied in a hushed tone, her voice as tired as the rest of her body. "Does this mean Casey Ray is dead?" she asked.

"Honestly, I think Casey Ray has been dead for a long time. As for Bas, I don't know for sure." answered Shura, the toll of the last few weeks clear on her face. "I stabbed her. I stabbed her in the side, but then she fled through a portal." Shura continued. She fell silent for a second, hiding her face with her hand as tears escaped down her soft skin. Alexandra moved Shura's hand aside, gently wiping her tears away. She had never seen Shura look so vulnerable, and for the first time since they had met, she looked incredibly young and afraid.

"If she comes back we'll be ready for her. And this time you won't be alone." Alexandra soothed. Shura hastily wiped the remainder of her tears from her cheeks.

"I almost forgot, I have something that belongs to you." Shura said, her voice wobbled with the sound of recent tears and emotion. She lifted something out of her pocket and placed it delicately into Alexandra's palm. Alexandra could feel the hum, the familiar beat in perfect time with her own heartbeat, and she felt a surge of strength ripple through her body. She felt safe as her Tairseach key vibrated subtly against the soft skin of her palm, as if her missing piece had been found and now she was whole again.

Epilogue

Alexandra and Shura stood atop the castle roof, looking out over the water. The sun had finally made an appearance, a signal that spring was just around the corner. The Cosantóirí were still yet to find a way to bring Hector back, and they were trying not to lose hope. Lexi had barely left her makeshift lab in the basement in the last few weeks, she was so determined to find a way to help Hector, and she had recruited Izzy as her new protégé. Raimund had taken up sparring with Skyler to keep him clean and focused, whilst Malandra tried to split her time between work and The Cosantóirí. Alexandra could feel the warmth of the sun gently caressing her bruised face, as if the sunlight was trying to heal her. She never imagined that this was where life would take her, as she watched the birds landing by the water. There was still no news on the status, or whereabouts, of Bas, a fact that kept Alexandra awake at night. The girl still haunted her dreams, and sometimes she could still feel the ropes around her wrists and ankles. Alexandra hoped that feeling would fade as the bruises did, and that her mind would heal as the broken bones did.

"You know, A.C., we are yet to go on an actual date." said Shura, the sun picking out the golden strands in her hair and making them sparkle.

"Well, I think it's time we changed that. Don't you?" Alexandra replied with a warm smile, placing her hand in

Shura's. "I mean, if you still want to after all of this craziness." Alexandra said shyly.

"Life without a little crazy would be incredibly boring." stated Shura simply, squeezing Alexandra's hand in return.

Zoe A. Jones

ABOUT THE AUTHOR

As an LGBT writer Zoe Jones seeks to promote positive representations of diverse characters. Zoe's debut novel *The Cosantóirí* places Alexandra Chadwick, a strong LGBT female lead, at the helm of the action packed adventure. With a background in psychology, criminology, and global governance Zoe has always been fascinated by people and places – both real and imagined.

Growing up in a small seaside town in Devon, Zoe was raised on tea and outdoor adventures. An upbringing that led to a love of running, rock climbing, and field hockey.

Lightning Source UK Ltd.
Milton Keynes UK
UKHW012002101220
374921UK00003B/794